Voices of Faith

Christian fiction, Volume 1

Gregory Allen Parker

Published by Graywolf Press, 2024.

This is a work of fiction. Similarities to real people, places, or events are entirely coincidental.

VOICES OF FAITH

First edition. August 3, 2024.

Copyright © 2024 Gregory Allen Parker.

ISBN: 979-8227166142

Written by Gregory Allen Parker.

Table of Contents

To those who walk by faith and not by sight, who find hope in the darkest moments and see the light in every corner of life. This book is dedicated to the unsung heroes of faith—the quiet believers whose lives are a testament to the power of prayer, love, and unwavering trust in God. May these stories inspire you as much as your faith inspires the world.

Chapter 1: The Miracle at Sunset

The village of Elmsworth nestled itself quietly among rolling hills and lush green fields. With a population that barely surpassed a few hundred, it was a place where everyone knew everyone else, and the rhythm of life was slow and steady. The heart of this small community was its church, a quaint stone building with a tall steeple that seemed to touch the sky. Every Sunday, the villagers gathered here, their voices lifting in unison to sing praises and offer prayers.

It was in this serene setting that young Lily Thompson lived. At just twelve years old, Lily was a beacon of light in the village. Her faith was as unwavering as the steeple that marked the heart of Elmsworth. She was known for her kind heart, always ready with a smile or a helping hand. Despite her tender age, Lily possessed a wisdom and spirituality that surpassed many of the older, more seasoned members of the congregation.

Lily lived with her grandmother, Mrs. Thompson, in a modest cottage at the edge of the village. Her parents had passed away in a tragic accident when she was just a baby, and her grandmother had raised her with love and devotion. Mrs. Thompson was a devout woman, and she instilled in Lily the same deep faith that had carried her through her own trials.

One late summer afternoon, as the sun dipped low on the horizon, casting a golden hue over the fields, a crisis began to unfold in Elmsworth. The village's only well, the primary source of water for everyone, had run dry. For weeks, the villagers had noticed the water level decreasing, but they had hoped it was just a temporary drought. Now, there was no denying it—there was no more water.

Panic began to ripple through the village. Without the well, they had no means to sustain themselves. The nearest town with a reliable water source was miles away, and many of the villagers were elderly or lacked the means to travel that far. Fear and uncertainty hung in the air like a dark cloud.

The village gathered in the square, murmuring among themselves, their faces etched with worry. Mrs. Thompson stood with Lily, holding her hand tightly. Lily could feel the fear emanating from her grandmother and the villagers around her.

The village elder, Mr. Collins, stepped forward to address the crowd. "My friends," he began, his voice steady but tinged with concern, "we are facing a serious situation. Our well has run dry, and we must find a solution. I propose we send a delegation to the nearest town to seek help. In the meantime, we must conserve what little water we have left."

As Mr. Collins continued to speak, Lily felt a stirring in her heart. She remembered a story her grandmother had told her many times, a story of faith and miracles. It was the story of Elijah and the widow of Zarephath, who, through unwavering faith, had seen a miracle that sustained them through a drought. Lily believed with all her heart that God could perform such a miracle for them, too.

She tugged at her grandmother's sleeve. "Grandma," she whispered, "we need to pray. We need to ask God for a miracle."

Mrs. Thompson looked down at Lily, her eyes filled with a mixture of fear and hope. She nodded slowly, understanding the depth of her granddaughter's faith. "You're right, Lily," she said softly. "We must pray."

Lily stepped forward, her small figure standing out against the backdrop of anxious faces. She raised her voice, clear and unwavering. "Mr. Collins, everyone, please, let's pray together. God can help us if we believe."

The villagers turned to look at Lily, their expressions a mix of skepticism and curiosity. But there was something about her conviction that made them pause. Mr. Collins nodded. "Lily is right. Let us pray."

The villagers formed a circle, holding hands, their heads bowed in prayer. Lily stood in the center, her hands clasped tightly, her eyes closed. She prayed with all her heart, asking God to provide for their needs, to send them a miracle just as He had done in the stories of old.

As they prayed, the sun began to set, casting a warm, golden light over the village. The sky was a brilliant canvas of oranges and pinks, the beauty of the sunset contrasting with the gravity of their situation. The prayer circle was silent, save for the murmured prayers and the soft rustling of leaves in the evening breeze.

Minutes turned into an hour, and still, they prayed. Just as the last rays of the sun were disappearing below the horizon, something extraordinary happened. A soft, cool breeze swept through the village square, carrying with it the scent of rain. The villagers opened their eyes, looking around in wonder.

In the distance, dark clouds were gathering, moving swiftly towards Elmsworth. The air was charged with anticipation as the first drops of rain began to fall. The drizzle quickly turned into a downpour, drenching the parched earth and filling the air with the refreshing scent of rain. The villagers stood in awe, their prayers answered in a way they had not expected.

Tears of joy and relief mingled with the rain on their faces. They laughed and hugged each other, their spirits lifted by the unexpected miracle. Lily stood with her grandmother, a radiant smile on her face. She knew, without a doubt, that God had heard their prayers.

The rain continued through the night, replenishing the dry well and bringing new life to the village. By morning, the crisis had passed, and the villagers gathered once more in the square, this time to give thanks.

Mr. Collins addressed the crowd again, his voice filled with emotion. "My friends, we have witnessed a miracle. Let us never forget the power of faith and the strength of our community. We must always remember to turn to God in our times of need."

Lily's faith had brought about an unexpected miracle, inspiring everyone around her to believe in the power of prayer. From that day forward, the village of Elmsworth was a testament to the power of faith and the miracles that could happen when people came together in prayer.

Years later, the story of the miracle at sunset would be told and retold, becoming a cherished part of the village's history. And at the heart of that story was a young girl whose unwavering faith had brought hope and inspiration to an entire community.

Chapter 2: The Prodigal Son Returns

In the bustling city of Newbridge, life moved at an electric pace. Skyscrapers pierced the sky, casting long shadows over the streets below, where the hum of traffic and the chatter of pedestrians created a symphony of urban existence. Amidst this modern cacophony lived a young man named Jacob Williams. He was the pride and joy of his family, having grown up in a loving household with strong Christian values. His parents, Thomas and Mary Williams, were well-respected in their community for their kindness, generosity, and unwavering faith.

Jacob had always been a bright and ambitious child. He excelled in school, was active in the church, and had dreams of making a difference in the world. However, as he reached his late teens, the allure of the city and the promise of freedom began to draw him away from the life he had known. The more he was exposed to the fast-paced world outside his family's influence, the more he yearned for independence and adventure.

By the time Jacob turned twenty-one, he felt suffocated by the expectations and constraints of his upbringing. He decided it was time to break free and chart his own course, far from the watchful eyes of his family and the familiarity of his faith. One evening, after a heated argument with his father about his future, Jacob made a drastic decision. He packed his belongings, took his savings, and left home without looking back.

The city welcomed Jacob with open arms. For the first time in his life, he felt the intoxicating rush of complete freedom. He rented a small apartment in a trendy neighborhood and quickly immersed himself in the vibrant nightlife. The days of structured routines and Sunday services were replaced with late nights at clubs, parties, and an endless stream of new faces.

Jacob found work at a marketing firm, where his natural charm and intelligence helped him climb the ranks quickly. His colleagues admired his drive and ambition, and soon he was living a life that many envied. But with success came excess. The money he earned was spent as quickly as it came, on luxurious dinners, designer clothes, and extravagant parties. His once modest lifestyle became a whirlwind of indulgence and hedonism.

As time passed, Jacob's connection to his family and faith grew more distant. Calls from his parents became infrequent, and his visits home ceased altogether. He convinced himself that he was happier this way, free from the constraints of his past. Yet, despite the outward appearances of success and contentment, a deep sense of emptiness began to creep into his soul.

One fateful night, after yet another lavish party, Jacob found himself alone in his apartment, the silence pressing in on him like a weight. He sat on his couch, surrounded by the trappings of his success, but feeling more isolated than ever. The life he had built, once so thrilling, now felt hollow and meaningless. He realized that in his quest for freedom, he had lost something far more valuable—his sense of purpose and belonging.

The following months were a downward spiral. Jacob's reckless lifestyle caught up with him. His work performance suffered, and his once-promising career began to falter. He found solace in alcohol and gambling, hoping to fill the void inside him. His savings dwindled, and soon he found himself in debt, with creditors hounding him relentlessly. The friends who had once flocked to his side disappeared, leaving him to face his troubles alone.

It was during this dark period that Jacob hit rock bottom. One cold winter night, after losing a significant amount of money in a poker game, he stumbled out of the casino and wandered the streets aimlessly. The neon lights and bustling crowds seemed to mock his misery. Desperate and broken, he collapsed on a park bench, tears streaming down his face. He thought about his family, the home he had abandoned, and the faith he had forsaken.

In that moment of despair, a memory surfaced—one of his mother, Mary, reading the parable of the prodigal son to him as a child. He remembered how she had explained the story, emphasizing the father's unconditional love and forgiveness. The memory pierced his heart, and for the first time in years, he prayed. It was a simple, heartfelt prayer, asking for guidance and a chance to make things right.

The next morning, Jacob woke up with a newfound clarity. He knew what he needed to do. It wouldn't be easy, and he wasn't sure if his family would even want to see him, but he had to try. With a heart full of both hope and trepidation, he made his way to the train station and bought a ticket to his hometown.

The journey back to Newbridge was a long and reflective one. As the cityscape gave way to familiar countryside, Jacob's mind raced with thoughts of the past and the future. He rehearsed what he would say to his parents, how he would apologize for the pain he had caused. Despite his fears, a small part of him held on to the hope that they would welcome him back, just as the father had welcomed the prodigal son in the parable.

When the train finally pulled into the station, Jacob took a deep breath and stepped onto the platform. The town looked much the same as he remembered, but it felt different, like a place from a distant dream. He made his way to his parents' house, the walk feeling both familiar and foreign. As he approached the front door, his heart pounded in his chest. With a trembling hand, he knocked.

The door opened, and there stood Thomas Williams. The years had added lines to his face and gray to his hair, but his eyes were the same—kind and steady. For a moment, father and son simply looked at each other, the weight of the past hanging between them.

"Dad," Jacob began, his voice choked with emotion, "I'm so sorry. I...I made so many mistakes. I don't know if you can ever forgive me, but I had to come back and try."

Thomas's eyes softened, and without a word, he stepped forward and pulled Jacob into a tight embrace. "Welcome home, son," he said, his voice thick with emotion. "We've missed you so much."

Tears streamed down Jacob's face as he clung to his father, the weight of his guilt and shame lifting in that moment of unconditional love. Thomas led him inside, where Mary was waiting. She rushed to her son, enveloping him in a warm hug, her tears mingling with his.

Over the next few days, Jacob shared his story with his parents, opening up about the highs and lows of his life in the city. They listened without judgment, their hearts full of compassion and understanding. They had never stopped praying for him, never stopped hoping that he would find his way back home.

Jacob's return to Newbridge was a time of healing and reconciliation. He reconnected with his faith, finding solace in the familiar rituals and teachings that had once been a cornerstone of his life. He attended church with his parents, seeking forgiveness and guidance. The congregation, many of whom had known him since childhood, welcomed him back with open arms, their support reinforcing his resolve to start anew.

With time, Jacob found ways to make amends for his past actions. He reached out to those he had wronged, offering apologies and seeking to rebuild broken relationships. He also began volunteering in the community, using his skills and experiences to help others who were struggling. His journey of redemption was not an easy one, but it was filled with moments of grace and growth.

One evening, as Jacob sat on the porch with his father, watching the sun set over the hills, he felt a deep sense of peace. He had come full circle, from the heights of ambition to the depths of despair, and back to the embrace of family and faith. His journey had taught him the true meaning of forgiveness, love, and the power of redemption.

"Dad," Jacob said softly, "thank you for believing in me, even when I didn't believe in myself."

Thomas smiled, placing a hand on his son's shoulder. "Jacob, you were always my son, no matter what. And just like the father in the parable, I knew that love and faith would bring you back home."

As the sun dipped below the horizon, casting a golden glow over the land, Jacob felt a renewed sense of purpose. He was no longer lost; he had found his way back to where he belonged. And with the support of his family and his faith, he knew he could face whatever challenges lay ahead.

The story of Jacob's return became a beacon of hope for many in Newbridge. It reminded them that no matter how far one strayed, redemption and forgiveness were always within reach. And in the quiet moments of reflection, Jacob would often think back to that night on the park bench, when a simple prayer had set him on the path to home.

Years later, as Jacob stood in the church, sharing his testimony with the congregation, he spoke of the transformative power of love and faith. His journey had come full circle, and his story served as a testament to the enduring message of the prodigal son—that no one is ever truly lost, and the door to redemption is always open.

Jacob's life, once filled with turmoil and regret, was now a testament to the power of second chances. His return had not only healed his own heart but had also strengthened the bonds within his family and community. And as he looked out at the faces of those who had supported him, he knew that he had found his true home, anchored in faith, love, and the unwavering belief in the power of redemption.

Chapter 3: The Guardian Angel

The city of Riverbend was known for its picturesque landscapes and tranquil river that wound its way through the heart of the town. But for Michael Hunter, Riverbend had become nothing more than a backdrop to his increasingly monotonous and unfulfilled life. At thirty-five, Michael found himself trapped in a job he despised, surrounded by people he couldn't relate to, and burdened by a growing sense of purposelessness. His faith, once a guiding force in his life, had faded to a distant memory.

Michael worked as an insurance claims adjuster, a job that paid the bills but offered little else. Each day, he trudged through stacks of paperwork and dealt with disgruntled clients, feeling as though he was merely going through the motions. The vibrant energy of his youth had been replaced by a dull resignation.

One rainy evening, after a particularly grueling day at work, Michael found himself stuck in traffic on the bridge that spanned the Riverbend River. The rain hammered down on his windshield, the rhythmic thumping of the wipers a stark contrast to the storm raging in his mind. He was lost in thoughts of his failed marriage, his estranged relationship with his family, and the gnawing void in his heart.

As he inched forward in the gridlock, his phone buzzed on the passenger seat. He glanced over and saw his ex-wife's name flashing on the screen. Sarah had been the love of his life, but their relationship had crumbled under the weight of unmet expectations and unresolved conflicts. The divorce had left him bitter and broken, and he had distanced himself from everyone, including God.

Michael sighed and ignored the call, focusing back on the road. The rain had turned the streets into a slick hazard, and he was anxious to get home. But fate had other plans. In a split second, he saw a car in the opposite lane lose control, skidding across the divider and heading straight towards him. There was no time to react. The impact was sudden and violent, metal crunching against metal, glass shattering, and then—darkness.

When Michael regained consciousness, he found himself lying on a hospital bed, the sterile smell of antiseptics filling his nostrils. His body ached all over, and his head throbbed with a dull pain. As he struggled to sit up, a nurse entered the room and gently guided him back down.

"Take it easy, Mr. Hunter," she said kindly. "You've been through a severe accident. You're lucky to be alive."

Michael groaned, trying to piece together the fragments of his memory. "What happened?"

"You were in a car accident. You suffered a concussion and several broken ribs. The doctors were worried about internal bleeding, but it looks like you're going to be okay."

He closed his eyes, the weight of his situation settling over him. "How long have I been here?"

"Three days. You were unconscious for most of it. Your family has been trying to reach you."

Family. The word felt foreign to him. He hadn't spoken to his parents or siblings in months, too ashamed of his failures to face them. "I don't want to see anyone right now," he muttered.

The nurse gave him a sympathetic look. "I understand. But maybe you should consider letting them in. You don't have to go through this alone."

Michael nodded weakly, not committing to anything. As the nurse left the room, he felt a deep sense of isolation. He had pushed everyone away, and now, lying in a hospital bed, he realized just how alone he truly was.

Later that night, as he lay staring at the ceiling, he heard a soft knock on the door. Before he could respond, the door opened, and a man stepped inside. He was tall and thin, with piercing blue eyes and an air of calmness that seemed to fill the room.

"Hello, Michael," the man said, his voice gentle yet firm. "My name is Gabriel."

Michael frowned, trying to place the face. "Do I know you?"

Gabriel smiled, a serene expression that made Michael feel strangely at ease. "No, we've never met. But I'm here to help you."

"Help me? With what?"

"With finding your way back."

Michael's confusion deepened. "Back to what?"

"Back to yourself. Back to faith. Back to the life you were meant to live."

Michael shook his head, wincing at the pain it caused. "I don't understand. Who are you, really?"

Gabriel pulled up a chair and sat beside the bed. "Think of me as a guardian angel. I'm here to guide you through this difficult time."

Michael couldn't help but scoff. "A guardian angel? Really? I'm not sure I believe in that kind of thing anymore."

Gabriel's eyes softened with compassion. "It's okay to be skeptical. But I promise you, I'm here for a reason. There's more to your life than the pain and emptiness you're feeling right now."

As the days passed, Gabriel visited Michael regularly, offering comfort and companionship. At first, Michael was wary, unsure of what to make of this mysterious stranger. But Gabriel's presence was soothing, and slowly, Michael began to open up.

They talked about everything—Michael's failed marriage, his strained relationship with his family, his disillusionment with his job, and his lost faith. Gabriel listened without judgment, his gentle guidance helping Michael to see his life from a new perspective.

"Why do you think your marriage failed?" Gabriel asked one afternoon, as they sat by the window, watching the rain.

Michael sighed, running a hand through his disheveled hair. "Sarah and I wanted different things. We stopped communicating. I think we both gave up too easily."

"Do you still love her?"

Michael hesitated, the old wounds still raw. "I don't know. Maybe. But I don't think she'd ever want to be with me again."

"Love is a powerful force, Michael. It can heal even the deepest wounds. But it requires faith and effort. Have you forgiven yourself for the mistakes you made?"

The question hit him hard. Forgiveness was something he hadn't considered. He had been so focused on his failures that he hadn't thought about the possibility of redemption.

"I don't know if I can," he admitted.

Gabriel placed a reassuring hand on his shoulder. "Forgiveness is a journey, not a destination. It starts with accepting that you're human and that mistakes are a part of life. It's about learning from them and growing."

As Michael reflected on Gabriel's words, he began to see the truth in them. He had been punishing himself for so long that he had forgotten how to move forward. With Gabriel's help, he started to confront his past, acknowledging the pain and regret but also recognizing the lessons they held.

One evening, as they walked through the hospital garden, Gabriel asked, "Do you remember the last time you felt truly at peace?"

Michael thought for a moment, his mind drifting back to a simpler time. "It was probably when I was a kid, at church with my family. There was something comforting about the rituals, the sense of community, the belief that there was something greater than myself."

"Faith can be a powerful anchor in times of turmoil," Gabriel said. "It's not about blind belief but about trust and surrender. It's about finding strength in the knowledge that you're never truly alone."

Michael nodded, feeling a flicker of something he hadn't felt in years—a glimmer of hope. "I used to pray all the time," he confessed. "But somewhere along the way, I lost that connection."

"It's never too late to reconnect," Gabriel encouraged. "Faith is always there, waiting for you to reach out."

Over the following weeks, Michael's physical condition improved, and so did his outlook on life. With Gabriel's guidance, he began to take small steps towards rebuilding his faith. He started reading the Bible again, finding solace in the familiar verses. He prayed, not out of desperation, but with a genuine desire to seek guidance and strength.

One morning, as Michael was preparing to be discharged from the hospital, Gabriel came to visit him one last time. "You're ready, Michael," he said with a warm smile. "Remember, this is just the beginning of your journey. Keep your heart open, and you'll find the path that was meant for you."

Michael felt a lump in his throat, a mixture of gratitude and sadness. "Thank you, Gabriel. I don't know how I would have gotten through this without you."

Gabriel's eyes twinkled with a mysterious light. "You're stronger than you realize, Michael. Never forget that. And remember, you are never alone."

As Gabriel left, Michael felt a profound sense of peace. He didn't fully understand who or what Gabriel was, but he knew that the encounter had changed him in ways he couldn't yet comprehend.

Returning home was both daunting and liberating. Michael's apartment, once a symbol of his isolation, now felt like a blank canvas, ready for a new beginning. He started making amends, reaching out to his family and friends, rebuilding the relationships he had neglected.

His parents were overjoyed to hear from him, their relief palpable. They welcomed him back into their lives with open arms, their unconditional love a testament to the power of family and forgiveness. His siblings, too, were supportive, understanding the struggles he had faced and the changes he was making.

Michael also reached out to Sarah. It was a difficult and emotional conversation, but it marked the beginning of a new chapter for both of them. While they didn't rush back into a relationship, they agreed to work on their friendship, to support each other in their respective journeys.

As the months passed, Michael found a renewed sense of purpose. He left his job at the insurance firm and pursued a career in counseling, inspired by his own experiences and his desire to help others. He became involved in his church once again, finding joy and fulfillment in serving his community.

One Sunday, as he sat in the pews, listening to the sermon, Michael felt a deep sense of gratitude. His journey had been arduous, but it had brought him back to a place of faith and hope. He thought about Gabriel and the profound impact the mysterious stranger had had on his life.

Michael knew that he still had a long way to go, but he was no longer afraid. He had learned that faith wasn't about having all the answers but about trusting the journey, finding strength in the face of adversity, and believing in the possibility of redemption.

Years later, as Michael shared his story with others, he spoke of Gabriel, the guardian angel who had guided him through his darkest days. His tale became a source of inspiration for many, a reminder that even in the midst of life's greatest challenges, there is always hope and the promise of divine intervention.

And so, the man who had once been lost found his way back, not through a sudden miracle, but through the quiet, unwavering presence of an angel who taught him the true meaning of faith and the power of second chances.

Chapter 4: Faith in the Storm

The small coastal town of Haven's Reach had always been a serene and idyllic place, a sanctuary for its inhabitants with its picturesque views of the Atlantic Ocean and the soothing sounds of waves crashing against the shore. The town's charm lay in its tight-knit community, where everyone knew each other, and the local church was the heart of the community. For the Wilson family, this church was more than just a place of worship; it was a cornerstone of their lives, a symbol of their faith and resilience.

John and Mary Wilson, along with their two children, Emily and Ben, had lived in Haven's Reach their entire lives. John was a carpenter, known for his meticulous craftsmanship and unwavering work ethic. Mary, a schoolteacher, was beloved by her students and known for her gentle yet firm demeanor. Their children, Emily, fifteen, and Ben, twelve, shared their parents' deep faith and love for their community.

The Wilsons' home was a modest but beautiful house situated just a few blocks from the beach. It was filled with warmth, love, and the comforting presence of faith. Every evening, the family gathered for dinner, followed by a prayer session where they expressed gratitude for their blessings and sought guidance for their challenges. This routine had been the bedrock of their lives, providing a sense of stability and continuity.

One summer evening, as the family sat down for dinner, John noticed a strange stillness in the air. The usual sounds of seagulls and the gentle rustling of the trees were absent, replaced by an eerie silence. As they bowed their heads for prayer, the faint sound of the town's emergency siren pierced the quiet, causing a ripple of concern to pass through the family.

John quickly turned on the radio, tuning in to the local news station. The voice of the weather forecaster, strained with urgency, filled the room. "We interrupt this program to bring you an important weather update. A

Category 4 hurricane, named Hurricane Gloria, is expected to make landfall near Haven's Reach within the next 24 hours. Residents are advised to evacuate immediately and seek shelter inland. This is a life-threatening situation. Please take all necessary precautions."

The Wilsons exchanged worried glances. Haven's Reach had experienced hurricanes before, but none had been predicted to be as severe as this one. The thought of leaving their home and everything they had built was daunting, but the safety of the family was paramount.

John turned to his family, his voice steady but filled with concern. "We need to prepare to leave. We'll gather our essentials and head to the community shelter inland."

Mary nodded, her expression resolute. "Let's stay calm and work together. God will guide us through this."

Emily and Ben, though anxious, drew strength from their parents' calm demeanor. They hurried to pack their belongings, focusing on the essentials—clothes, important documents, and a few cherished items. Mary gathered food and water supplies, while John secured the house as best as he could, boarding up windows and reinforcing doors.

As they worked, the reality of the impending storm loomed over them. The sky darkened, and the wind began to pick up, howling through the trees and sending debris swirling through the air. The normally tranquil ocean now roared with ferocity, waves crashing violently against the shore.

By the time they were ready to leave, the storm's outer bands had already begun to lash the town. The rain pelted down in sheets, and the wind howled like a relentless beast. The family hurried to their car, their movements deliberate but swift. John drove carefully through the increasingly treacherous conditions, navigating fallen branches and rising water levels.

As they approached the community shelter, the scene was chaotic. Families were arriving in droves, seeking refuge from the storm. Volunteers and emergency personnel directed them to safety, their faces etched with concern and determination. The Wilsons joined the throngs of people inside the shelter, finding a spot to settle amidst the crowd.

The shelter, a large gymnasium, buzzed with a mix of fear and hope. Families huddled together, comforting one another and praying for safety. The Wilsons joined a group prayer led by Pastor Daniels, the local church's pastor.

His voice, though calm, carried the weight of the collective anxiety and hope of the community.

"Dear Lord," Pastor Daniels began, "we come to you in this time of need, seeking your protection and guidance. We trust in your plan and your infinite wisdom. Give us strength and courage to face the storm ahead, and watch over our homes and loved ones. Amen."

The prayer brought a sense of unity and calm to the shelter. As the storm outside intensified, the people inside drew closer together, their faith a beacon of light in the darkness.

Hours passed, and the storm raged with unrelenting fury. The shelter shook with the force of the wind, and the sounds of debris crashing against the building echoed through the space. Despite the chaos outside, the Wilsons remained steadfast, their faith unwavering. They comforted one another, shared stories, and prayed for their town.

As dawn approached, the storm began to subside. The winds weakened, and the rain lessened, leaving behind a landscape that had been battered and bruised. The community shelter, though shaken, had withstood the storm, a testament to the strength and resilience of its construction and the people within it.

With the worst of the storm over, the residents of Haven's Reach emerged from the shelter to survey the damage. The town they loved had been ravaged by Hurricane Gloria. Streets were flooded, homes were damaged, and trees were uprooted. The once serene beach was now a scene of devastation, littered with debris.

The Wilsons returned to their home, their hearts heavy with anticipation. As they turned onto their street, they saw that their house, though battered, was still standing. The preparations John had made had helped to mitigate some of the damage, but it was clear that extensive repairs would be needed.

John and Mary held each other tightly, their relief palpable. "Thank God we're safe," Mary whispered.

John nodded, his eyes misty with emotion. "We'll rebuild. Together, we'll get through this."

The days that followed were a testament to the strength and resilience of the Haven's Reach community. Neighbors helped one another, sharing resources and offering support. The church became a hub of activity, coordinating relief efforts and providing a place of solace and hope.

The Wilsons were at the forefront of these efforts, their faith guiding them through the challenges. John used his carpentry skills to help repair homes, while Mary organized food drives and offered comfort to those in need. Emily and Ben, inspired by their parents' example, volunteered their time to assist with cleanup and support their friends.

Despite the hardships, the community's faith remained unshaken. They held onto the belief that God had a plan for them, and that through their collective strength and trust in His guidance, they would emerge stronger.

One evening, as the Wilsons gathered for their family prayer, John spoke from the heart. "We've faced a great trial, but our faith has carried us through. Let's continue to trust in God's plan and support one another. Together, we can rebuild and find hope in the midst of adversity."

As they bowed their heads in prayer, a sense of peace settled over them. They had weathered the storm, and though the path ahead was uncertain, their faith and resilience would light the way.

Months passed, and Haven's Reach slowly began to recover. Homes were rebuilt, businesses reopened, and the community's spirit remained unbroken. The Wilsons' home, once a symbol of their struggle, now stood as a testament to their perseverance and faith.

One Sunday, the church held a special service to give thanks for their survival and to honor the efforts of those who had worked tirelessly to rebuild the town. The pews were filled with familiar faces, all united in their gratitude and hope for the future.

Pastor Daniels stood at the pulpit, his voice filled with emotion as he addressed the congregation. "We have faced a great storm, but through our faith and unity, we have emerged stronger. Let us continue to support one another, to trust in God's plan, and to find hope in His infinite love."

The congregation responded with a heartfelt "Amen," their voices a chorus of resilience and faith.

After the service, the Wilsons stood together outside the church, looking out at the town they loved. Emily and Ben held their parents' hands, their faces filled with pride and hope.

"We did it," Ben said softly. "We made it through."

Mary smiled, her eyes shining with tears. "Yes, we did. And we'll continue to face whatever comes our way, together."

John nodded, his heart full of gratitude. "Our faith has seen us through the storm, and it will guide us as we rebuild and look to the future."

As the sun set over Haven's Reach, casting a golden glow over the town, the Wilsons knew that their journey was far from over. But with their unwavering faith and the support of their community, they were ready to face whatever challenges lay ahead.

Their story, a testament to the strength and resilience that comes from trusting in God's plan, would inspire others for years to come. And as they stood together, their hearts full of hope and determination, they knew that they were not alone. They had each other, their faith, and a community that would always stand by them, no matter the storm.

IN THE DAYS AND WEEKS that followed, Haven's Reach continued its journey of recovery. The community, now bonded even more tightly by their shared experience, worked tirelessly to restore their town. Fundraisers, volunteer efforts, and countless acts of kindness became the new normal, showcasing the best of humanity in the face of adversity.

One particularly memorable event was the "Rebuild Haven's Reach" festival, organized by the town to raise funds and

celebrate their progress. The festival was held in the town square, adorned with handmade decorations and filled with booths offering food, crafts, and games. Music filled the air, and laughter echoed through the streets—a stark contrast to the eerie silence of the stormy night months before.

The Wilsons played a significant role in organizing the festival. Mary coordinated with local vendors and ensured that there was something for everyone to enjoy. John and Emily built stages and booths, while Ben helped with setting up and running games for the kids.

The highlight of the festival was a special performance by the church choir, which had been practicing for weeks. Their voices, raised in harmony, sang songs of hope and resilience, moving many in the crowd to tears. It was a moment of collective healing, a reminder of the strength they had found in their faith and each other.

As the sun set on the festival, the community gathered for a final prayer, led by Pastor Daniels. "Dear Lord," he began, his voice strong and filled with gratitude, "we thank you for the strength and resilience you have given us. We thank you for the love and support of our community. As we continue to rebuild, we ask for your guidance and blessings. Amen."

The "Amen" that followed was a powerful affirmation of their shared faith and determination.

In the months that followed, the Wilsons continued to be pillars of their community. Their home, now fully repaired, became a gathering place for friends and neighbors, a symbol of hope and perseverance. John expanded his carpentry business, using his skills to help others rebuild and strengthen their homes. Mary, inspired by the resilience of her students, started a mentorship program to support children affected by the hurricane.

Emily and Ben, having witnessed the power of faith and community firsthand, became active members of the youth group at church, organizing events and volunteering their time to help others. Their experiences during and after the hurricane had shaped them, instilling a deep sense of empathy and responsibility.

One year after Hurricane Gloria, the town held a remembrance service to honor those who had been affected and to celebrate their recovery. The service was held at the beach, where the town had first felt the fury of the storm. It was a beautiful day, the sky clear and the ocean calm, a stark contrast to the chaos of the previous year.

The Wilsons stood together, their hearts full of gratitude. As Pastor Daniels led the congregation in prayer, they held hands, feeling the strength of their faith and the support of their community.

"Dear Lord," Pastor Daniels prayed, "we thank you for bringing us through the storm. We thank you for the resilience and strength you have given us. As we look to the future, we ask for your continued guidance and blessings. May we always remember the power of faith and the strength of our community. Amen."

As the congregation echoed the "Amen," the Wilsons looked out at the ocean, a symbol of the challenges they had faced and the hope that lay ahead.

They knew that their journey was far from over, but with their unwavering faith and the support of their community, they were ready for whatever came next.

Their story, a testament to the strength and resilience that comes from trusting in God's plan, would continue to inspire others for years to come. And as they stood together, their hearts full of hope and determination, they knew that they were not alone. They had each other, their faith, and a community that would always stand by them, no matter the storm.

Chapter 5: The Healing Touch

The small town of Maplewood was a place where life moved at a gentle, unhurried pace. Nestled among rolling hills and verdant forests, it was a community bound by strong ties of friendship and faith. At the heart of this close-knit town stood St. Andrew's Church, a modest but beautiful building with a tall steeple that could be seen from miles around. For many, St. Andrew's was more than just a place of worship; it was a sanctuary, a source of strength, and a beacon of hope.

For Rebecca Hayes, St. Andrew's had always been a central part of her life. A dedicated member of the church, Rebecca was known for her kindness, her unwavering faith, and her beautiful singing voice, which often led the congregation in hymns. However, in recent years, Rebecca's life had taken a difficult turn. Diagnosed with a chronic illness that left her in constant pain and fatigue, she had struggled to maintain her usual active role in the church and the community.

Rebecca's illness, fibromyalgia, was a condition characterized by widespread pain, sleep problems, fatigue, and often emotional and mental distress. It had no known cure and was difficult to manage, leading to a significant decline in her quality of life. The once vibrant and energetic woman found herself battling constant discomfort and exhaustion, her days marked by a relentless struggle to simply get through.

The support of her family and friends had been a lifeline for Rebecca, but even their love and care couldn't fully alleviate her suffering. Her husband, David, was a pillar of strength, always by her side, but she could see the worry in his eyes and the toll it was taking on him. Their children, Emma and Lucas, tried to help in any way they could, but it pained Rebecca to see how her illness affected them.

One Sunday morning, as Rebecca sat in the pews of St. Andrew's, she felt particularly overwhelmed by her condition. The physical pain was one thing, but the emotional and spiritual toll was another. She had always been a woman of strong faith, but the constant struggle had begun to erode her sense of hope. As she listened to the choir sing, her mind drifted to thoughts of despair and doubt.

After the service, Pastor Jonathan approached her with a warm smile. "Rebecca, it's good to see you here today. How have you been holding up?"

Rebecca forced a smile, not wanting to burden him with her troubles. "I'm managing, Pastor. It's just been a rough few weeks."

Pastor Jonathan's eyes softened with understanding. "I know it's been difficult, Rebecca. But remember, you are not alone. We are all here for you, and so is God. Have you considered joining our prayer group? We meet every Wednesday evening to pray for those in need of healing and support."

Rebecca hesitated. She had always been a private person, preferring to keep her struggles to herself. But something in Pastor Jonathan's words resonated with her. Perhaps the collective strength of the church community could help her find some solace.

"I'll think about it," she said finally, her voice barely above a whisper.

Pastor Jonathan placed a reassuring hand on her shoulder. "We would love to have you join us. Sometimes, sharing our burdens with others can lighten the load. Remember, God works through the love and support of His people."

That evening, Rebecca sat in her living room, contemplating Pastor Jonathan's invitation. She knew she needed help, but the idea of opening up about her pain and struggles to others felt daunting. She glanced at a framed photograph on the mantelpiece—a picture of her family, taken during happier times. The smiles on their faces were a stark contrast to the current reality, and a pang of longing surged through her.

"Maybe it's time to let others in," she thought to herself. With a sense of determination, she decided to attend the prayer group the following Wednesday.

When the day arrived, Rebecca felt a mix of apprehension and hope. As she entered the church hall, she was greeted by warm smiles and friendly faces. The group consisted of about a dozen members, each with their own stories of struggle and faith. Pastor Jonathan welcomed her warmly and introduced her to the group.

"Everyone, this is Rebecca. She's been a member of our church for many years, and she's here to join us in prayer and support."

The group responded with kind words and nods of encouragement. Rebecca felt a sense of relief wash over her. Maybe this was what she needed—a community of people who understood the power of prayer and were willing to support her through her journey.

The prayer group began with a hymn, followed by individual prayers and testimonies. As Rebecca listened to the others share their stories, she realized that she was not alone in her struggles. Each person had their own battles, yet their faith remained unshaken. It was inspiring and humbling.

When it was her turn to speak, Rebecca took a deep breath and began to share her story. She spoke of her diagnosis, the constant pain, the emotional toll, and the strain it had put on her family. Tears welled up in her eyes as she spoke, but she felt a weight lifting off her shoulders with each word.

The group listened with empathy and compassion. When she finished, Pastor Jonathan led the group in a special prayer for Rebecca, asking for God's healing touch and strength to carry her through her struggles. The collective prayers and the sense of community enveloped her like a warm embrace.

As the weeks went by, Rebecca continued to attend the prayer group. The support and prayers of the group members became a source of strength and comfort. She found herself looking forward to the meetings, where she could share her burdens and find solace in the collective faith of the group.

One evening, after a particularly uplifting session, Pastor Jonathan approached Rebecca with an idea. "Rebecca, I know you've been struggling with your illness, but I've noticed how much you light up when you sing. Your voice is a gift, and I think it could bring a lot of joy and healing to others. How would you feel about leading a special music ministry for those in need of hope and comfort?"

Rebecca was taken aback by the suggestion. She had always loved singing, but her illness had made it difficult to find the energy and motivation. However, the idea of using her voice to help others resonated deeply with her.

"I don't know, Pastor. I'm not sure if I have the strength for it," she admitted.

Pastor Jonathan smiled warmly. "You don't have to do it alone. We can support you, and you can start small. Sometimes, using our gifts to help others can bring healing to ourselves as well."

Rebecca mulled over the idea for a few days, praying for guidance. The more she thought about it, the more she felt a sense of purpose stirring within her. Perhaps this was a way to channel her pain into something meaningful, to find healing through helping others.

With renewed determination, Rebecca agreed to lead the music ministry. She began by organizing small gatherings at the church, inviting people who were struggling with illness, loss, or other challenges. She chose songs that spoke of hope, faith, and God's love, and as she sang, she poured her heart and soul into the music.

The response was overwhelming. People found comfort and strength in her voice, and the gatherings became a source of healing for many. Rebecca's own spirit began to lift, and she felt a sense of connection and purpose that she hadn't experienced in a long time.

One evening, after a particularly moving session, a woman named Margaret approached Rebecca with tears in her eyes. "Rebecca, your singing has brought me so much peace. I've been struggling with my own health issues, and your music has been a balm to my soul. Thank you for sharing your gift with us."

Rebecca hugged Margaret, her heart swelling with gratitude. "Thank you, Margaret. Your words mean so much to me. I'm just grateful that I can use my voice to bring a little light into the darkness."

As the music ministry grew, Rebecca's health began to show signs of improvement. The prayers and support of the church community, combined with the sense of purpose she found in helping others, brought a renewed strength to her body and spirit. While her illness was still a part of her life, it no longer defined her. She had found a way to live with it, to rise above it, and to use her experience to bring hope to others.

One Sunday, as Rebecca stood in front of the congregation to lead a special hymn, she looked out at the faces of her family, friends, and fellow church members. The love and support she saw reflected in their eyes filled her with a profound sense of gratitude. She had come full circle, from a place of despair to a place of hope and healing.

As she sang, her voice strong and clear, she felt the presence of God enveloping her, guiding her, and giving her the strength to continue her journey. The words of the hymn resonated deeply within her soul:

"Great is Thy faithfulness, O God my Father;

There is no shadow of turning with Thee;

Thou changest not, Thy compassions, they fail not;

As Thou hast been, Thou forever wilt be."

Tears streamed down Rebecca's face as she sang, not from pain or sorrow, but from a deep sense of peace and joy. She had found her way back to faith, to community, and to a sense of purpose. And in doing so, she had discovered the true power of healing—the healing touch of God's love, made manifest through the prayers and support of her church community.

As the final notes of the hymn echoed through the church, the congregation rose to their feet in a standing ovation. Rebecca looked out at the sea of smiling faces and felt a profound sense of connection. She was not alone in her journey. She had the support of her family, her friends, and her faith.

After the service, as people came up to express their gratitude and share their own stories of struggle and hope, Rebecca felt a deep sense of fulfillment. She had found her calling, a way to use her gifts to bring comfort and healing to others. And in doing so, she had found healing for herself.

The music ministry continued to grow, becoming a vital part of St. Andrew's Church. Rebecca's voice, once silenced by pain and despair, now rang out with hope and joy, a testament to the power of faith and community. Her journey was far from over, but she faced each day with a renewed sense of strength and purpose.

Years later, as Rebecca looked back on her journey, she saw it not as a story of suffering, but as a story of resilience, faith, and the transformative power of love. Her illness had been a catalyst for growth, pushing her to find new ways to connect with others and to deepen her faith.

Rebecca's story became an inspiration to many, a reminder that even in the darkest of times, there is always hope. Through the prayers and support of her church community, she had found a way to rise above her pain and to use her experiences to bring light to others.

And so, the woman who had once been defined by her illness became a beacon of hope, her voice a healing touch that reached out to those in need.

Rebecca Hayes had found her way back to faith, and in doing so, she had discovered the true meaning of healing—the power of love, faith, and the unwavering support of a community bound together by God's grace.

AS THE YEARS PASSED, Rebecca's influence continued to grow. Her music ministry expanded beyond the walls of St. Andrew's Church, reaching neighboring towns and communities. She began to receive invitations to sing at various events, conferences, and gatherings, where she shared her story and her songs of hope and faith.

Rebecca also found herself mentoring others who were struggling with chronic illnesses. She started a support group, offering a safe space for people to share their experiences, find comfort in each other's company, and draw strength from their collective faith. The group met regularly at St. Andrew's, and it quickly became a source of solace and inspiration for many.

One of the most memorable moments in Rebecca's journey came when she was invited to speak and sing at a national conference for chronic illness awareness. The event brought together people from all walks of life, each with their own stories of struggle and resilience. Rebecca's message of hope and the healing power of faith resonated deeply with the audience.

As she stood on the stage, her voice filling the large auditorium, Rebecca felt a profound sense of purpose. She knew that her journey had brought her to this moment, where she could use her voice to inspire and uplift others. Her heart swelled with gratitude for the path she had walked, and for the unwavering support of her church community that had carried her through.

After her performance, Rebecca was approached by numerous people who shared their own stories and expressed their gratitude for her message. One woman, named Sarah, stood out in particular. Sarah was in her early thirties and had been diagnosed with multiple sclerosis. She was struggling to cope with the physical and emotional toll of the disease.

"Rebecca, your story and your songs have given me so much hope," Sarah said, her eyes filled with tears. "I've been feeling so lost and alone, but hearing you speak and sing has reminded me that I'm not alone, and that there is always hope."

Rebecca took Sarah's hands in hers, offering a warm smile. "You are never alone, Sarah. God is with you every step of the way, and so are we. There is strength in community and in faith. Never lose hope."

The connection between Rebecca and Sarah marked the beginning of a deep friendship. Sarah joined Rebecca's support group and became an active member of the music ministry. Together, they continued to spread the message of hope and healing, touching countless lives along the way.

Rebecca's journey also brought her closer to her family. David, Emma, and Lucas had been her rock, supporting her through every challenge. As they witnessed Rebecca's transformation and the impact of her ministry, their own faith deepened. The family grew closer, united by their shared experiences and their collective faith.

One sunny afternoon, the Wilson family gathered for a picnic in the park. As they sat together, enjoying the warmth of the sun and the beauty of nature, Rebecca reflected on how far they had come.

"Do you remember those difficult days when my illness seemed overwhelming?" Rebecca asked, looking at her family with gratitude.

David nodded, his eyes filled with love. "I do, Rebecca. But look at where we are now. Your strength and faith have brought us through those dark times and into the light."

Emma, now a young woman with a strong sense of purpose, added, "Mom, you've taught us the importance of faith and community. You've shown us that even in the face of great challenges, there is always hope."

Lucas, who had grown into a thoughtful and compassionate young man, chimed in, "We're so proud of you, Mom. Your journey has inspired us all to be better and to have faith, no matter what."

Rebecca smiled, her heart full of love and gratitude. "I couldn't have done it without all of you. Your support and love have been my greatest source of strength. And our faith has carried us through."

As the sun began to set, casting a golden glow over the park, the Wilson family joined hands and bowed their heads in prayer. They thanked God for the blessings they had received, for the strength to face their challenges, and for the love that bound them together.

"Dear Lord," Rebecca prayed, her voice steady and filled with emotion, "we thank you for your guidance and your grace. We thank you for the strength to overcome our struggles and for the love that surrounds us. As we continue our journey, may we always remember to have faith and to support one another. Amen."

As they echoed the "Amen," the Wilson family felt a deep sense of peace and unity. They had weathered the storm together, and their faith had been their anchor. Rebecca's journey of healing had brought them closer, and their love for one another had grown stronger.

In the years that followed, Rebecca's influence continued to expand. She wrote a book about her experiences, sharing her story of faith, resilience, and the healing power of community. The book, titled "The Healing Touch: A Journey of Faith and Hope," became a source of inspiration for many, reaching people far beyond the small town of Maplewood.

Rebecca also continued to lead the music ministry and the support group, both of which grew in size and impact. She traveled to various communities, sharing her message and her music, and touching the lives of countless individuals who were struggling with their own challenges.

Through it all, Rebecca remained grounded in her faith and her community. St. Andrew's Church continued to be a source of strength and support, and her family remained her rock. Together, they faced each new challenge with hope and resilience, knowing that they were never alone.

Rebecca's journey was a testament to the power of faith, love, and community. It was a reminder that even in the darkest of times, there is always hope, and that through the support of others, we can find the strength to heal and to thrive.

And so, the woman who had once been defined by her illness became a beacon of hope and inspiration. Her voice, a healing touch that reached out to those in need, continued to bring light to the world. Rebecca Hayes had found her way back to faith, and in doing so, she had discovered the true meaning of healing—the power of love, faith, and the unwavering support of a community bound together by God's grace.

Chapter 6: The Power of Forgiveness

The small town of Brooksville was a picturesque place, nestled between rolling hills and a winding river. Its charm lay in its tight-knit community, where everyone knew each other, and the local church was a cornerstone of daily life. Among the residents of Brooksville were two siblings, Samuel and Rachel Carter, who had once been inseparable but had drifted apart over the years due to a series of misunderstandings and unresolved conflicts.

Samuel, the elder by three years, had always been the more responsible and pragmatic of the two. After their parents passed away in a tragic accident, he took on the role of guardian and provider for his younger sister. He worked tirelessly to keep their family farm running, often sacrificing his own dreams and aspirations in the process. Rachel, on the other hand, was spirited and independent, determined to carve out her own path. She left Brooksville shortly after high school to pursue a career in the city, leaving Samuel to shoulder the burden of the farm alone.

Over the years, the physical distance between them grew into an emotional chasm. Samuel felt abandoned and resentful, while Rachel struggled with guilt and regret for leaving her brother behind. Their sporadic attempts at communication often ended in arguments, deepening the rift between them. Neither of them realized how much their unresolved issues were affecting their lives and their faith.

One summer, after a particularly heated argument over the phone, Rachel decided to return to Brooksville. She had recently lost her job and was facing a personal crisis, prompting her to seek solace in the familiar comforts of home. Despite her apprehensions, she knew she needed to confront the past and attempt to mend her relationship with Samuel.

Rachel arrived in Brooksville on a warm afternoon, the town looking much the same as she remembered. She felt a mix of nostalgia and anxiety as she drove down the familiar streets, eventually pulling up to the family farm. The sight of the farmhouse brought back a flood of memories—both happy and painful.

Samuel was in the barn when Rachel arrived. He was tending to the horses, his expression weary and distracted. When he saw her, a mixture of surprise and wariness crossed his face.

"Rachel," he said, his voice guarded. "What brings you back?"

Rachel took a deep breath, steeling herself. "I needed to come home, Samuel. We need to talk."

Samuel's jaw tightened. "There's nothing to talk about. You've made your choices, and I've made mine."

"Please, Samuel," Rachel implored. "Can we just sit down and talk? For once, without arguing?"

Samuel hesitated, the hurt and resentment clear in his eyes. But he nodded, wiping his hands on a rag and gesturing for her to follow him to the house.

They sat at the kitchen table, the silence between them heavy with unspoken words. Rachel glanced around, noting how little had changed. The same curtains, the same worn-out furniture, the same sense of home that she had missed.

"I'm sorry for leaving, Samuel," Rachel began, her voice trembling. "I know it was selfish, and I've regretted it every day. I didn't realize how much it would hurt you, how much it would hurt us."

Samuel's expression softened slightly, but the pain was still evident. "You left me to handle everything on my own, Rachel. I felt like you didn't care about the farm, about me. You just walked away."

"I did care," Rachel insisted. "I still do. I was just...lost. I wanted to find myself, to live my own life. But I never stopped thinking about you, about home."

Samuel sighed, rubbing his temples. "I don't know, Rachel. It's been so long. We've both changed."

"Maybe we have," Rachel agreed. "But that doesn't mean we can't find our way back to each other. We were always stronger together. Don't you remember?"

Samuel looked at his sister, seeing the sincerity in her eyes. He remembered the bond they once shared, the laughter, the support, the love. Maybe it wasn't too late to salvage what they had lost.

"Alright," he said finally. "Let's try to talk, to really talk."

Over the next few days, Samuel and Rachel began to rebuild their relationship, one conversation at a time. They reminisced about their childhood, shared their struggles and triumphs, and slowly began to understand each other's perspectives. It wasn't easy, and there were still moments of tension and disagreement, but they were both committed to healing the wounds of the past.

One Sunday, Rachel suggested they attend church together. Samuel was hesitant at first, having drifted away from his faith over the years, but he agreed. The service at Brooksville Community Church was a familiar comfort, the hymns and prayers a reminder of simpler times.

Pastor Evans, a kind and wise man who had known the Carter family for years, noticed the siblings sitting together. After the service, he approached them with a warm smile.

"It's good to see you both here," Pastor Evans said. "How have you been, Samuel? Rachel?"

"We're...working on things," Samuel replied, glancing at Rachel.

Rachel nodded. "It's been a long time, Pastor. But we're trying to find our way back to each other."

Pastor Evans placed a hand on Samuel's shoulder. "Forgiveness and reconciliation are powerful acts of faith. It takes courage to face the past and to seek healing. Remember, God is with you on this journey."

Rachel felt a surge of hope at Pastor Evans' words. She knew that their path to forgiveness would be challenging, but she believed that with faith and perseverance, they could mend their relationship.

As the weeks turned into months, Samuel and Rachel continued to work on their relationship. They spent time together on the farm, rediscovering their shared love for the land and the simple joys of country life. They laughed, they cried, and they prayed together, slowly rebuilding the trust and connection they had lost.

One evening, as they sat on the porch watching the sunset, Rachel turned to Samuel with a thoughtful expression. "Do you ever think about Mom and Dad?" she asked softly.

"All the time," Samuel replied. "I miss them every day."

"Me too," Rachel said, her voice breaking. "I wish they were here to see us now, to see that we're trying to make things right."

Samuel reached out and took her hand, a gesture of comfort and solidarity. "I think they'd be proud of us, Rachel. Proud that we're finding our way back to each other."

Rachel nodded, tears in her eyes. "I think so too. And I think they'd want us to forgive ourselves, as well as each other."

Samuel squeezed her hand, his own eyes misty. "You're right. Forgiveness isn't just about the other person. It's about letting go of the guilt and the pain, and finding peace."

That night, as Rachel lay in bed, she felt a sense of peace she hadn't known in years. The journey to forgiveness and reconciliation was far from over, but she knew they were on the right path. With God's guidance and the support of their community, they could heal the wounds of the past and build a stronger, more loving relationship.

The following Sunday, during the church service, Pastor Evans gave a sermon on forgiveness. His words resonated deeply with Samuel and Rachel, reinforcing the importance of their journey.

"Forgiveness is not an easy path," Pastor Evans said. "It requires humility, courage, and faith. It means letting go of the hurt and resentment, and opening our hearts to healing and reconciliation. But it is through forgiveness that we find true peace and freedom."

After the service, Samuel and Rachel approached Pastor Evans, thanking him for his words of wisdom and support. The pastor embraced them both, his eyes filled with warmth and encouragement.

"Remember, forgiveness is a process," Pastor Evans said. "It's a journey, not a destination. But with each step you take, you are moving closer to healing and wholeness. Trust in God's grace and in the strength of your love for each other."

As the weeks went by, Samuel and Rachel continued to deepen their bond. They faced challenges and setbacks, but they faced them together, with a renewed sense of faith and commitment. They found solace in their church community, drawing strength from the prayers and support of their friends and neighbors.

One sunny afternoon, Samuel and Rachel decided to visit their parents' graves, a pilgrimage they had both been avoiding for years. The cemetery was a peaceful place, nestled on a hillside overlooking the town. The sight of their parents' headstones brought a wave of emotion, but also a sense of closure.

As they stood together, Samuel spoke softly. "Mom, Dad, we miss you so much. We're trying to honor your memory by healing our relationship. We're finding our way back to each other, and to God."

Rachel knelt beside the graves, her heart filled with love and gratitude. "Thank you for everything you taught us, for the love and the faith you instilled in us. We promise to carry those lessons forward, and to support each other as you would have wanted."

They spent the afternoon sharing memories and reflecting on their journey. The visit to the cemetery became a turning point, a moment of healing and reconciliation that strengthened their resolve to move forward together.

In the months that followed, Samuel and Rachel's relationship continued to flourish. They found joy in the simple moments, like tending to the garden, cooking meals together, and taking long walks through the fields. They also became more involved in their church, leading Bible study groups and volunteering for community service projects.

Their journey of forgiveness and reconciliation also inspired others in the community. Friends and neighbors who had witnessed their struggles and their healing found hope and encouragement in their story. Samuel and Rachel's journey became a testament to the power of faith, love, and forgiveness.

One Sunday, Pastor Evans invited Samuel and Rachel to share their story with the congregation. As they stood before the church, they felt a mixture of nerves and gratitude. Samuel spoke first, his voice steady and heartfelt.

"Rachel and I have been through a lot together," he began. "We've faced misunderstandings, resentment, and years of separation. But through it all, we've learned the true meaning of forgiveness. It's not just about letting go of the past, but about opening our hearts to healing and reconciliation. It's about trusting in God's grace and finding strength in our faith and in each other."

Rachel continued, her voice filled with emotion. "Forgiveness is a journey, and it's not always easy. But it's a journey worth taking. It's brought Samuel and me closer together, and it's helped us find peace and joy in our lives. We want to thank all of you for your prayers and support. You've been a part of our healing, and we are forever grateful."

The congregation responded with a standing ovation, their applause a testament to the power of Samuel and Rachel's story. It was a moment of celebration and affirmation, a reminder that forgiveness and reconciliation were possible through faith and love.

As Samuel and Rachel looked out at the faces of their friends and neighbors, they felt a deep sense of fulfillment. Their journey had been challenging, but it had also been transformative. They had found their way back to each other and to God, and they were stronger for it.

In the years that followed, Samuel and Rachel continued to build their lives together, grounded in their faith and their love for each other. They faced new challenges and joys, but they faced them with the strength and resilience they had gained through their journey of forgiveness.

Their story became a lasting legacy in Brooksville, a reminder of the power of faith, love, and forgiveness. It inspired others to seek reconciliation in their own lives, to find healing through the grace of God and the support of their community.

And so, the siblings who had once been estranged found their way back to each other, their hearts united by the power of forgiveness. Their journey was a testament to the enduring strength of faith and the transformative power of love. Samuel and Rachel Carter had discovered the true meaning of forgiveness, and in doing so, they had found peace, joy, and a deeper connection with God and each other.

As they stood together on the family farm, watching the sun set over the hills, they knew that their journey was far from over. But they faced the future with hope and determination, knowing that they were never alone. They had each other, their faith, and the unwavering support of their community.

Their story, a beacon of hope and inspiration, would continue to light the way for others, a testament to the power of forgiveness and the boundless grace of God. And as they walked hand in hand into the future, Samuel and Rachel knew that they had truly found their way home.

Chapter 7: A Light in the Darkness

The city of Fairview was a bustling metropolis, its streets alive with the ceaseless flow of people and traffic. Amidst the noise and chaos, it was easy to overlook the less fortunate, those who lived in the shadows of society. Among them was a man named Daniel, who had been homeless for several years. Life on the streets was harsh and unforgiving, a daily struggle for survival that left little room for hope.

Daniel had once been a successful accountant, with a comfortable home and a loving family. But a series of unfortunate events—a failed business venture, the death of his wife, and a battle with depression—had led him down a path of despair. He lost his job, his home, and eventually his connection to the world he once knew. The streets of Fairview became his new reality, a place where he felt invisible and forgotten.

Winter in Fairview was particularly brutal. The icy wind cut through the thin layers of clothing Daniel wore, and the biting cold seeped into his bones. Finding shelter was a constant challenge, and the few resources available to the homeless were often stretched to their limits. Daniel's days were consumed with the search for food, warmth, and a safe place to sleep.

One particularly cold evening, as Daniel huddled in a doorway to escape the wind, he noticed a man walking towards him. The man was dressed in a long coat and scarf, his breath visible in the frosty air. He approached Daniel with a warm smile, his eyes filled with genuine concern.

"Hello there," the man said, extending a hand. "My name is Pastor Mark. What's your name?"

Daniel hesitated, unsure of the stranger's intentions. "Daniel," he replied cautiously.

"It's nice to meet you, Daniel," Pastor Mark said, his voice kind and reassuring. "Are you hungry? I have some food I'd like to share with you."

Daniel's stomach growled in response, and he nodded. Pastor Mark handed him a brown paper bag, the aroma of freshly made sandwiches wafting from it. Daniel accepted the bag gratefully, his hands trembling from the cold.

"Thank you," Daniel said, his voice barely above a whisper.

Pastor Mark sat down beside him, seemingly unbothered by the cold concrete beneath them. "You're welcome, Daniel. There's a shelter a few blocks from here, run by our church. It's warm, and we have hot meals and beds. You're welcome to come with me if you'd like."

Daniel looked at Pastor Mark, his eyes searching for any hint of deceit or ulterior motive. But all he saw was genuine kindness and a desire to help. With a mixture of reluctance and hope, he nodded.

"Alright," Daniel said. "I'll come with you."

The walk to the shelter was short, but it felt like a journey of a thousand miles to Daniel. Pastor Mark walked beside him, asking gentle questions about his life and listening intently to his answers. For the first time in a long while, Daniel felt seen and heard.

The shelter was a modest building, its walls adorned with murals painted by local artists. Inside, the warmth was a stark contrast to the frigid streets outside. The air was filled with the comforting smell of hot food, and the sound of people talking and laughing created a sense of community.

"Welcome to St. James Shelter," Pastor Mark said as they entered. "This is a place where you can rest and find some comfort. Let me introduce you to some of the staff."

Pastor Mark led Daniel to a small office where a woman was busy organizing supplies. "This is Sarah, our shelter coordinator. She'll help you get settled in."

Sarah looked up and smiled warmly at Daniel. "Hi, Daniel. It's nice to meet you. Let's get you something warm to drink and find you a bed."

Daniel followed Sarah to the dining area, where he was given a steaming cup of coffee and a bowl of hearty stew. The simple act of sitting at a table, eating a hot meal, and feeling the warmth of the shelter was overwhelming. Tears filled his eyes as he realized how much he had missed these basic comforts.

After finishing his meal, Sarah showed Daniel to a small, clean bed in one of the dormitory rooms. The mattress was firm but inviting, and a warm blanket was neatly folded at the foot of the bed. As Daniel lay down, the weight of exhaustion and cold seemed to lift from his body. For the first time in a long while, he felt safe.

That night, Daniel slept deeply, his dreams filled with images of his past life and a faint glimmer of hope for the future. When he awoke the next morning, the sun was shining through the small window, casting a warm glow over the room. He took a deep breath, feeling a sense of peace he hadn't known in years.

Over the next few days, Daniel settled into a routine at the shelter. He helped with chores, attended the communal meals, and participated in group activities. Pastor Mark and the staff at St. James Shelter made him feel welcome and valued, offering not just physical support but also emotional and spiritual guidance.

One afternoon, as Daniel was helping to serve lunch, Pastor Mark approached him with a thoughtful expression. "Daniel, would you be interested in joining our weekly Bible study group? It's a small gathering where we discuss scripture and share our thoughts and experiences. I think you might find it helpful."

Daniel hesitated. It had been a long time since he had engaged with his faith, and he wasn't sure if he was ready to revisit that part of his life. But the kindness and support he had received at the shelter made him consider the possibility.

"Alright," Daniel said finally. "I'll give it a try."

The Bible study group met in a cozy room at the back of the shelter. A circle of chairs surrounded a small table, on which rested a well-worn Bible. Pastor Mark led the group, which consisted of a few other shelter residents and some volunteers from the church.

As they began to read and discuss passages from the Bible, Daniel felt a sense of familiarity and comfort. The words of scripture resonated with him in a way they hadn't before, and he found himself drawn into the discussions, sharing his thoughts and listening to the experiences of others.

One evening, Pastor Mark shared a passage from the Book of Matthew: "Come to me, all you who are weary and burdened, and I will give you rest." The words struck a chord with Daniel, bringing tears to his eyes.

"That's how I've felt for so long," Daniel admitted. "Weary and burdened. I lost everything that mattered to me, and I didn't know how to find my way back."

Pastor Mark nodded, his eyes filled with compassion. "We all carry burdens, Daniel. But through faith and the support of others, we can find rest and healing. God loves you, and He is always with you, even in the darkest times."

The words of Pastor Mark and the support of the Bible study group began to transform Daniel's outlook on life. He started to reconnect with his faith, finding solace in prayer and scripture. The sense of community at St. James Shelter gave him a renewed sense of purpose and belonging.

As winter turned to spring, Daniel's life continued to improve. He found part-time work at a local grocery store, which helped him regain a sense of independence and stability. The staff at the shelter supported him every step of the way, providing resources and encouragement.

One sunny afternoon, as Daniel was walking through the park on his way to work, he came across a group of children playing soccer. The sight brought a smile to his face, and he was reminded of the joy and innocence of his own childhood. As he watched, one of the children kicked the ball too hard, sending it rolling towards him.

Daniel picked up the ball and walked over to the group. "Looks like you lost something," he said with a grin, handing the ball back to the child.

"Thanks, mister!" the child replied with a big smile.

As Daniel continued on his way, he felt a sense of happiness and contentment that had been missing from his life for so long. He realized that the simple acts of kindness and connection were what made life meaningful.

That evening, during Bible study, Pastor Mark shared a passage from the Book of James: "Faith without works is dead." The group discussed the importance of living out their faith through actions and service to others.

Daniel listened intently, feeling a growing sense of conviction. He wanted to give back, to help others as he had been helped. After the session, he approached Pastor Mark with an idea.

"Pastor, I've been thinking. I'd like to volunteer here at the shelter, to help others who are going through what I went through. Is there a way I can do that?"

Pastor Mark's face lit up with a smile. "Absolutely, Daniel. We'd be grateful for your help. Your experience and compassion will make a real difference in the lives of others."

Daniel began volunteering at the shelter, assisting with meal preparation, organizing supplies, and offering support to new residents. His own journey of transformation gave him a unique perspective and empathy for those who were struggling. He became a source of encouragement and hope, sharing his story and listening to the stories of others.

One evening, as Daniel was helping to serve dinner, a new resident arrived at the shelter. The man, named Thomas, looked weary and defeated, much like Daniel had when he first arrived. Daniel approached him with a warm smile.

"Welcome to St. James Shelter, Thomas. My name is Daniel. If you need anything, just let me know."

Thomas looked at Daniel with a mix of skepticism and gratitude. "Thanks, Daniel. I don't know what to expect. I just...I don't know where else to go."

"I understand," Daniel said gently. "I've been there. This place can be a fresh start, a place to find hope and support. You're not alone."

As the days went by, Daniel took Thomas under his wing, offering guidance and companionship. He shared his own story of struggle and transformation, helping Thomas see that change was possible. The bond they formed was a testament to the power of compassion and community.

Through his volunteer work, Daniel also deepened his relationship with Pastor Mark. They often had long conversations about faith, life, and the importance of serving others. Pastor Mark's wisdom and kindness had been a guiding light for Daniel, and he was grateful for the friendship they had developed.

One afternoon, as they sat in the park enjoying the spring sunshine, Daniel turned to Pastor Mark with a thoughtful expression.

"Pastor, I've been thinking a lot about my faith and the journey I've been on. I feel like I've been given a second chance, and I want to make the most of it. But sometimes, I still struggle with the guilt and regret of my past. How do I move forward?"

Pastor Mark smiled gently. "Daniel, it's natural to have those feelings. But remember, God's grace is infinite. He forgives us, and He wants us to forgive ourselves. It's through forgiveness that we find true freedom and peace. Focus on the present and the future, on the good you can do and the lives you can touch."

Daniel nodded, taking the words to heart. "Thank you, Pastor. Your guidance has meant so much to me. I want to live a life that reflects the love and compassion I've received."

As the months turned into years, Daniel's life continued to flourish. He found a permanent job at the grocery store, eventually earning a promotion to assistant manager. He saved enough money to rent a small apartment, a place he could call his own. The sense of stability and accomplishment filled him with pride.

Daniel also remained deeply involved with St. James Shelter. He became a key volunteer, helping to organize events, mentor new residents, and share his story of transformation. His journey inspired others, showing them that change was possible and that hope could be found even in the darkest times.

One summer, St. James Shelter held a special event to celebrate the success stories of its residents and volunteers. The community gathered in the park, enjoying food, music, and fellowship. Pastor Mark took the stage to share a few words.

"Today, we celebrate the power of compassion, faith, and community," Pastor Mark said, his voice filled with emotion. "We honor those who have found their way back from the darkness and those who have supported them on their journey. One of those individuals is Daniel, whose story is a testament to the transformative power of love and kindness."

The crowd erupted in applause as Daniel stepped onto the stage. He felt a mix of humility and gratitude, overwhelmed by the support and encouragement of his community.

"Thank you," Daniel began, his voice steady but filled with emotion. "I am incredibly grateful for the kindness and support I have received here at St. James Shelter. When I first arrived, I was lost and broken. But through the love and compassion of this community, I found hope and a second chance at life."

He paused, looking out at the faces of those who had become his friends and family. "I want to thank Pastor Mark for his unwavering support and guidance. His actions showed me the love of Christ and helped me find my faith again. And to everyone here, thank you for believing in me and for the countless acts of kindness that have made a difference in my life."

As Daniel stepped down from the stage, the applause continued, a powerful affirmation of his journey and the impact he had made. He felt a deep sense of fulfillment, knowing that his story had touched the lives of others and that he had found a purpose in serving his community.

In the years that followed, Daniel continued to thrive. He remained a dedicated volunteer at St. James Shelter, his compassion and empathy touching the lives of countless individuals. He also deepened his faith, finding strength and guidance in prayer and scripture.

Daniel's journey of transformation was not without its challenges, but he faced each obstacle with resilience and faith. He knew that he was never alone, that the support of his community and the grace of God would carry him through.

One winter evening, as Daniel walked through the streets of Fairview, he came across a man huddled in a doorway, much like he had been years ago. The man looked up, his eyes filled with despair and hopelessness.

"Hey there," Daniel said, extending a hand. "My name is Daniel. Are you hungry? I have some food I'd like to share with you."

The man hesitated, then nodded slowly. Daniel handed him a brown paper bag, the aroma of freshly made sandwiches wafting from it.

"Thank you," the man said, his voice barely above a whisper.

Daniel smiled warmly. "You're welcome. There's a shelter a few blocks from here, run by our church. It's warm, and we have hot meals and beds. You're welcome to come with me if you'd like."

The man looked at Daniel with a mixture of skepticism and hope. Daniel saw himself in those eyes, remembering the kindness and support that had transformed his life.

"I'd like that," the man said finally.

As they walked towards St. James Shelter, Daniel felt a deep sense of purpose and gratitude. He knew that he was not just helping another person in need, but continuing the legacy of compassion and love that had been shown to him.

That evening, as Daniel and the new resident settled into the warmth of the shelter, he felt a profound sense of fulfillment. His journey had come full circle, and he was now a light in the darkness for others.

Through his actions and support, Daniel had discovered the true meaning of the love of Christ—a love that was selfless, compassionate, and transformative. It was a love that had the power to heal, to restore, and to bring hope to even the darkest of times.

And so, the homeless man who had once been lost and broken found his way back to a life filled with purpose, faith, and love. Daniel's story was a testament to the power of compassion and the light that could shine through even the darkest of circumstances. His journey continued, a beacon of hope and inspiration to all who crossed his path.

Chapter 8: The Faithful Widow

Elizabeth Graham had lived in the small town of Willowbrook for most of her life. The town was a quaint, picturesque place where everyone knew each other, and life moved at a gentle, predictable pace. Elizabeth and her husband, Robert, had shared a beautiful life together for over thirty years. They were a beloved couple in the community, known for their kindness, generosity, and unwavering faith. Robert was a local doctor, and Elizabeth had dedicated her life to supporting him and raising their two children, Margaret and Thomas, who were now grown and living in different cities.

But life had taken a sudden and heartbreaking turn when Robert was diagnosed with cancer. Despite a courageous battle, he passed away within six months, leaving Elizabeth reeling from the loss. The days following Robert's death were a blur of grief and numbness. Friends and family offered their condolences and support, but nothing could fill the void left by the man who had been her partner, confidant, and best friend.

Elizabeth found herself alone in the house they had shared, surrounded by memories of their life together. Every corner of the house reminded her of Robert—the worn armchair where he used to read, the garden they had tended together, the photos of their family that adorned the walls. The weight of her grief was overwhelming, and she struggled to find a reason to get out of bed each morning.

One Sunday morning, a few weeks after Robert's funeral, Elizabeth decided to attend church. It was a place that had always brought her comfort, and she hoped that being surrounded by her faith community would offer some solace. As she entered the familiar sanctuary of Willowbrook Community Church, she was greeted by warm smiles and gentle hugs from friends who were genuinely concerned for her well-being.

Pastor David, a kind and compassionate man who had been a friend of the Graham family for many years, noticed Elizabeth's presence and approached her with a sympathetic smile. "Elizabeth, it's good to see you here. How are you holding up?"

Elizabeth managed a small, sad smile. "It's been difficult, Pastor. I feel so lost without Robert."

Pastor David nodded, his eyes filled with understanding. "Grief is a heavy burden to bear, but remember that you are not alone. God is with you, and so are we. If you ever need to talk or pray, I'm here for you."

"Thank you, Pastor," Elizabeth replied, her voice trembling. "I appreciate that."

The service that morning was focused on finding strength and hope in difficult times. The hymns and prayers brought a sense of comfort to Elizabeth, and Pastor David's sermon resonated deeply with her. He spoke about the power of faith to carry us through our darkest moments and the importance of finding purpose even in the midst of grief.

"God has a plan for each of us," Pastor David said. "Even when we feel lost and broken, He is there, guiding us and giving us strength. Trust in Him, and you will find the light in the darkness."

As Elizabeth listened to his words, she felt a flicker of hope ignite within her. She realized that she needed to find a way to move forward, to honor Robert's memory by living a life filled with purpose and service. It wouldn't be easy, but she knew that her faith could guide her through this journey.

In the days that followed, Elizabeth began to take small steps towards healing. She spent more time in prayer, seeking comfort and guidance from God. She also reached out to her children, sharing her feelings and drawing strength from their love and support. Margaret and Thomas were worried about their mother, but they were also inspired by her resilience and determination to find a way through her grief.

One afternoon, as Elizabeth was tending to the garden that she and Robert had lovingly nurtured together, she had an idea. She remembered how much joy they had found in growing fresh vegetables and flowers, and she wondered if she could use the garden to bring some of that joy to others. With renewed determination, she decided to create a community garden, a place where people could come together, grow their own food, and find solace in the beauty of nature.

Elizabeth shared her idea with Pastor David, who was enthusiastic and supportive. "I think that's a wonderful idea, Elizabeth. The community garden could be a place of healing and connection for many people. How can we help you get started?"

With the church's support, Elizabeth began to plan the community garden. She reached out to friends and neighbors, inviting them to join her in this new endeavor. Many people were excited about the idea and eager to help. They donated seeds, tools, and their time to transform a vacant lot near the church into a thriving garden.

As the garden began to take shape, Elizabeth felt a renewed sense of purpose. She poured her energy into the project, finding solace in the physical work and the companionship of others. The garden became a place of healing, not just for Elizabeth, but for everyone who participated. People from all walks of life came together, sharing their stories, their hopes, and their faith.

One of the first to join Elizabeth in the garden was a young woman named Sarah. Sarah had recently moved to Willowbrook and was struggling to find her place in the community. She had lost her job and was feeling isolated and uncertain about her future. When she heard about the community garden, she decided to get involved, hoping that it would be a way to meet new people and find some stability.

As Sarah and Elizabeth worked side by side, they formed a deep bond. Sarah admired Elizabeth's strength and resilience, and Elizabeth found comfort in Sarah's youthful energy and optimism. They shared their stories and supported each other through their respective challenges.

One evening, as they were planting seedlings together, Sarah turned to Elizabeth with a thoughtful expression. "Elizabeth, I don't know if I've ever told you this, but working in this garden has changed my life. I was feeling so lost and alone before I met you. But now, I feel like I have a purpose and a community. Thank you for creating this space."

Elizabeth smiled warmly, her heart filled with gratitude. "Thank you, Sarah. You've been a blessing to me as well. This garden has given me a reason to keep going, a way to honor Robert's memory. I'm so glad it's brought you comfort too."

The community garden continued to flourish, attracting more people who were seeking a sense of connection and purpose. It became a place of beauty and abundance, a testament to the power of faith and community. Elizabeth found joy in seeing the garden grow and in witnessing the positive impact it had on others.

As the months went by, Elizabeth also found herself becoming more involved in other church activities. She joined a Bible study group, where she found comfort and inspiration in the scriptures and the support of her fellow members. She also volunteered at the church's food pantry, helping to provide for those in need.

One day, while volunteering at the food pantry, Elizabeth met a woman named Maria. Maria was a single mother struggling to make ends meet, and she had come to the pantry for help. Elizabeth could see the weariness in Maria's eyes and the weight of her burdens.

"Hi, Maria," Elizabeth said warmly. "I'm Elizabeth. How can I help you today?"

Maria hesitated, her eyes filling with tears. "I don't know where to start. It's just been so hard. I can't seem to get ahead, no matter how hard I try."

Elizabeth reached out and gently took Maria's hand. "I understand, Maria. Life can be incredibly challenging, but you're not alone. We're here to support you. Let's see what we can do to help."

As they talked, Elizabeth learned more about Maria's situation and offered her practical advice and emotional support. She also invited Maria to join the community garden, hoping that it would provide her with a sense of purpose and connection.

Maria accepted the invitation and soon became a regular at the garden. She found solace in the physical work and in the companionship of others who were facing their own challenges. Elizabeth and Maria formed a close bond, supporting each other through their respective journeys.

One Sunday, during a particularly moving church service, Pastor David spoke about the importance of serving others and finding purpose in faith. His words resonated deeply with Elizabeth and Maria, reinforcing their commitment to helping those in need.

"God calls us to be His hands and feet," Pastor David said. "To show love and compassion to those who are struggling, to be a light in the darkness. When we serve others, we are serving Him."

After the service, Elizabeth and Maria talked about the sermon and their shared commitment to serving others. They decided to organize a community outreach program, bringing together members of the church and the community to provide support and resources to those in need.

The outreach program was a success, drawing in volunteers from all walks of life. They provided meals, clothing, and other essentials to families in need, and offered support and encouragement to those facing difficult times. Elizabeth and Maria found fulfillment and joy in their work, knowing that they were making a positive impact on the lives of others.

As Elizabeth continued to serve her community, she felt a deep sense of purpose and connection. Her grief over Robert's loss was still present, but it was no longer the defining aspect of her life. Through her faith and her commitment to serving others, she had found a way to honor his memory and to move forward with hope and determination.

One evening, as Elizabeth was walking through the garden, she paused to reflect on her journey. The garden was in full bloom, a vibrant tapestry of colors and life. She felt a sense of peace and gratitude, knowing that she had found a way to navigate her grief and to make a difference in the lives of others.

As she stood there, Pastor David approached her with a smile. "Elizabeth, the garden looks beautiful. You've done an incredible job here."

"Thank you, Pastor," Elizabeth replied. "It's been a labor of love, and it's brought me so much joy and healing. I couldn't have done it without the support of the church and the community."

Pastor David nodded. "You've been an inspiration to all of us, Elizabeth. Your faith and your commitment to serving others have touched so many lives. You've shown us the true meaning of faithfulness and resilience."

Elizabeth felt a surge of emotion at his words. "I couldn't have done it without my faith, Pastor. It's what has carried me through the darkest times and given me the strength to keep going. And I'm so grateful for the support of this community. It's been a lifeline for me."

Pastor David placed a hand on her shoulder. "You've turned your grief into something beautiful, Elizabeth. You've found a way to honor Robert's memory and to bring hope to others. That's a powerful testament to the strength of your faith."

As Elizabeth continued her walk through the garden, she felt a renewed sense of purpose and determination. She knew that her journey was far from over, but she also knew that she had the strength and the faith to face whatever lay ahead. Through her grief, she had discovered the power of love, community, and faith, and she was committed to using that power to make a positive difference in the world.

In the months that followed, Elizabeth's community outreach program continued to grow and thrive. She worked tirelessly to provide support and resources to those in need, drawing strength from her faith and the support of her fellow volunteers. The community garden remained a place of beauty and healing, a testament to the power of nature and the strength of the human spirit.

One day, while working in the garden, Elizabeth received a visit from a young woman named Hannah. Hannah was a college student who had recently experienced a personal crisis and was struggling to find her way. She had heard about the community garden and hoped that it would provide her with some solace and direction.

"Hi, Elizabeth," Hannah said shyly. "My name is Hannah. I've been going through a tough time, and I was wondering if I could help out in the garden. I think it might be good for me."

Elizabeth smiled warmly, recognizing the pain and uncertainty in Hannah's eyes. "Of course, Hannah. We'd love to have you join us. Working in the garden has been incredibly healing for me, and I'm sure it will be for you too."

As Hannah began to work in the garden, she found comfort in the physical activity and the companionship of the other volunteers. Elizabeth took her under her wing, offering guidance and support as Hannah navigated her own journey of healing and self-discovery.

One evening, as they were planting new flowers together, Hannah turned to Elizabeth with a thoughtful expression. "Elizabeth, I don't know how to thank you. Being here has helped me more than I can say. I was feeling so lost, but now I feel like I have a purpose again."

Elizabeth's heart swelled with gratitude. "I'm so glad to hear that, Hannah. This garden has been a source of healing for many of us. It's a reminder that even in the darkest times, there is always hope and beauty to be found."

Hannah nodded, her eyes filled with emotion. "You've shown me that it's possible to find strength and purpose even in the midst of pain. Thank you for being such an inspiration."

As the sun set over the garden, casting a warm golden light over the flowers, Elizabeth felt a deep sense of peace and fulfillment. She had found a way to navigate her grief and to use her faith to make a positive impact on the lives of others. Her journey had been challenging, but it had also been incredibly rewarding.

In the years that followed, Elizabeth continued to serve her community with unwavering dedication. She remained a pillar of strength and compassion, drawing from the wellspring of her faith to support those in need. The community garden and outreach program thrived under her leadership, providing hope and healing to countless individuals.

Elizabeth's story became an inspiration to many, a testament to the power of faith, resilience, and the human spirit. Through her grief, she had discovered a new purpose and had touched the lives of so many with her kindness and compassion.

As she looked back on her journey, Elizabeth knew that she had found a way to honor Robert's memory and to live a life filled with purpose and love. Her faith had carried her through the darkest times, and she had emerged stronger and more determined than ever to make a difference in the world.

And so, the faithful widow who had once been overwhelmed by grief found her way to healing and purpose through her faith and her commitment to serving others. Elizabeth Graham's story was a beacon of hope and inspiration, a reminder that even in the face of loss and pain, there is always a light in the darkness, guiding us forward.

Chapter 9: The Missionary's Journey

The remote village of Kalumba nestled in the heart of the African savannah, far removed from the conveniences and bustle of modern life. The village was a world unto itself, defined by traditions passed down through generations, a close-knit community, and an enduring connection to the land. For Hannah Stevens, a young missionary from the United States, Kalumba represented both a challenge and an opportunity. She had come to this distant place with a deep sense of calling, ready to spread the gospel and offer help to the community.

Hannah's journey to Kalumba began months earlier, in the small town of Millbrook where she grew up. Raised in a devout Christian family, Hannah had always felt a strong connection to her faith. Her parents, both active members of their church, had instilled in her the values of compassion, service, and unwavering faith. After graduating from college with a degree in international studies, Hannah decided to dedicate her life to missionary work. She joined a mission organization and spent a year preparing for her journey—learning about different cultures, studying languages, and deepening her theological knowledge.

When the opportunity to serve in Kalumba arose, Hannah felt an undeniable pull. The village, she was told, had limited access to education, healthcare, and other basic services. The local church, though small and struggling, was eager for support. Hannah's heart went out to the people of Kalumba, and she committed herself to bringing them not just the message of the gospel, but also practical help and love.

After a long flight and a bumpy ride over dirt roads, Hannah finally arrived in Kalumba. The village was a cluster of thatched-roof huts surrounded by fields and open savannah. The air was thick with the scents of cooking fires and the sounds of children playing. Hannah's arrival was met with a mixture of curiosity and warmth. The villagers, though wary of outsiders, welcomed her with open hearts and open minds.

One of the first people Hannah met was Pastor James, the local church leader. Pastor James was a tall, soft-spoken man in his early forties, with a gentle demeanor and a deep love for his community. He had been serving in Kalumba for over a decade, often struggling against the odds to keep the church alive.

"Welcome, Hannah," Pastor James said, greeting her with a warm smile and a firm handshake. "We've been praying for you and are grateful for your willingness to join us."

"Thank you, Pastor James," Hannah replied, her heart swelling with gratitude. "I'm honored to be here and to serve alongside you."

Pastor James showed Hannah to a small, modest hut that would be her home for the next year. It was simple but cozy, with a bed, a small table, and a lantern for light. As she settled in, Hannah couldn't help but feel a sense of excitement and anticipation. She knew that her journey would be challenging, but she was ready to embrace it with an open heart and a steadfast faith.

The next day, Hannah began her work in earnest. She spent the morning with Pastor James, visiting families in the village and getting to know the community. The people of Kalumba were warm and welcoming, eager to share their stories and their lives with her. Hannah was struck by their resilience and their strong sense of community, despite the many hardships they faced.

In the afternoons, Hannah taught English and basic literacy skills to the children of the village. The school was a simple structure with a thatched roof and dirt floor, but it was filled with eager young faces and the sound of laughter. The children's enthusiasm and thirst for knowledge were infectious, and Hannah found immense joy in teaching them.

Evenings in Kalumba were a time of fellowship and worship. The small church, built of mud bricks and thatch, was the heart of the community. Hannah joined Pastor James and the villagers for nightly services, where they sang hymns, read scripture, and shared testimonies. The services were simple but deeply moving, filled with heartfelt prayers and a palpable sense of God's presence.

As the weeks turned into months, Hannah faced a myriad of challenges. The physical conditions were often harsh, with extreme heat, limited access to clean water, and the constant threat of disease. There were days when she felt exhausted and overwhelmed, questioning her ability to make a difference. But through it all, her faith remained unshaken.

One particularly difficult day, Hannah found herself struggling with a deep sense of inadequacy. A severe drought had hit the region, leaving the fields parched and the villagers desperate for water. The church had been working tirelessly to provide relief, but the needs were overwhelming.

As she sat in her hut, tears of frustration streaming down her face, Pastor James knocked on the door and entered. He saw her distress and sat down beside her, offering a comforting presence.

"Hannah, I can see that you're struggling," Pastor James said gently. "This work is not easy, and there are times when we all feel overwhelmed. But remember, we are not alone. God is with us, guiding us and giving us strength."

Hannah wiped her tears and looked at Pastor James, her heart aching with the weight of her emotions. "I just feel so helpless sometimes. There's so much need, and I don't know if I'm making a difference."

Pastor James smiled softly. "You are making a difference, Hannah. Every act of kindness, every lesson taught, every prayer shared—these things matter. They plant seeds of hope and faith that will grow over time. Trust in God's plan and know that your efforts are not in vain."

His words brought a sense of comfort and clarity to Hannah's heart. She realized that her role was not to solve every problem, but to be a vessel of God's love and grace. With renewed determination, she continued her work, trusting that God would use her efforts to bring about positive change.

One of the most rewarding aspects of Hannah's journey was witnessing the growth and transformation of the villagers. She saw the children's literacy skills improve, their faces lighting up with pride as they learned to read and write. She saw families coming together to support one another, their bonds strengthened by faith and community. And she saw the church grow in numbers and in spirit, becoming a beacon of hope for the entire village.

One evening, during a particularly powerful worship service, a young man named Samuel stood up to share his testimony. Samuel had been one of the village's most troubled youths, often getting into fights and causing trouble. But over the past few months, he had experienced a profound change, thanks in part to Hannah's influence and the support of the church.

"Before I met Hannah and Pastor James, I was lost," Samuel began, his voice filled with emotion. "I didn't see any hope for my future, and I didn't know if God cared about me. But through their kindness and their teachings, I've found a new path. I've found faith and a sense of purpose. I want to live my life for God and to help others find the same hope that I've found."

The congregation erupted in applause and praise, their hearts lifted by Samuel's powerful testimony. Hannah felt a deep sense of gratitude and awe, knowing that God was working through her to touch the lives of others.

As the service continued, Pastor James spoke about the importance of perseverance and faith in the face of challenges. He shared a passage from the Book of James: "Consider it pure joy, my brothers and sisters, whenever you face trials of many kinds, because you know that the testing of your faith produces perseverance. Let perseverance finish its work so that you may be mature and complete, not lacking anything."

Hannah reflected on these words, feeling a renewed sense of strength and determination. She knew that her journey was far from over, but she was ready to face whatever challenges lay ahead with faith and resilience.

One of the most challenging moments of Hannah's journey came when a cholera outbreak swept through the village. The disease spread rapidly, and the villagers were terrified. Hannah and Pastor James worked tirelessly to provide medical care, clean water, and education on hygiene practices to prevent further spread.

Despite their efforts, many villagers fell ill, and the church was turned into a makeshift clinic. Hannah spent long hours caring for the sick, administering rehydration solutions, and praying for healing. The sight of so much suffering weighed heavily on her heart, but she remained steadfast in her faith.

One night, as she sat by the bedside of a young girl named Miriam who was gravely ill, Hannah felt a deep sense of helplessness. Miriam's condition was worsening, and Hannah feared she might not survive. She held Miriam's hand and prayed fervently for God's intervention.

"Dear Lord, please heal Miriam. Give her strength and restore her health. We trust in Your power and Your mercy. Please bring comfort and peace to her and her family."

As she prayed, she felt a comforting presence, a sense of peace that reassured her that God was with them. She continued to care for Miriam throughout the night, her heart filled with hope and faith.

By morning, Miriam's condition began to improve. Her fever subsided, and she started to regain her strength. Hannah was filled with gratitude and awe, knowing that God had answered their prayers. Miriam's recovery brought hope to the entire village, and the cholera outbreak eventually came under control.

The experience strengthened Hannah's faith and deepened her commitment to serving the people of Kalumba. She realized that her journey was not just about spreading the gospel, but also about living out the teachings of Christ through acts of love, compassion, and service.

As the months turned into a year, Hannah's time in Kalumba was drawing to a close. She had formed deep bonds with the villagers, and saying goodbye was bittersweet. She had grown to love the community and had found a sense of purpose and fulfillment in her work.

On her last night in the village, the church held a special service to honor Hannah and to celebrate the impact she had made. The church was filled with people, their faces illuminated by the soft glow of lanterns. The air was thick with emotion as they sang hymns and offered prayers of gratitude.

Pastor James stood before the congregation, his voice filled with warmth and admiration. "Tonight, we gather to give thanks for Hannah's presence among us. Her dedication, compassion, and unwavering faith have touched our lives in ways that words cannot fully express. She has been a shining example of Christ's love, and we are forever grateful for her service."

Hannah felt tears welling up in her eyes as she listened to Pastor James' words. She stood and faced the congregation, her heart overflowing with love and gratitude.

"Thank you, Pastor James, and thank you to everyone in Kalumba. This past year has been one of the most challenging and rewarding experiences of my life. Your warmth, resilience, and faith have inspired me beyond measure. I will carry your stories, your faces, and your spirit with me always. I believe that God brought us together for a reason, and I am grateful for the opportunity to serve alongside you."

The congregation responded with a heartfelt chorus of "Amen," their voices echoing through the night. After the service, there was a gathering outside the church, with food, music, and laughter. The villagers presented Hannah with a handmade quilt, each square stitched with love and representing different aspects of their community. It was a gift that symbolized their gratitude and the bonds they had formed.

As the evening drew to a close, Hannah took a moment to reflect on her journey. She had faced numerous challenges, from the physical hardships to the emotional struggles of being far from home. But through it all, her faith had been her anchor, guiding her and giving her strength. She had witnessed the power of God's love in action and had seen how faith could transform lives, including her own.

Leaving Kalumba was not the end of her journey, but a new beginning. She knew that her experiences in the village had prepared her for whatever lay ahead. She felt a renewed sense of purpose and a deep commitment to continue serving others, wherever God might lead her.

As she boarded the plane the next morning, Hannah looked out over the vast savannah, feeling a sense of peace and gratitude. She knew that the seeds of hope and faith she had planted in Kalumba would continue to grow and flourish, just as they had in her own heart.

In the months and years that followed, Hannah continued her missionary work, serving in different parts of the world. She carried with her the lessons and experiences from Kalumba, drawing strength from the memories of the people she had met and the love they had shared.

Her journey was filled with new challenges and new opportunities to spread the gospel and to live out her faith. She found joy and fulfillment in each new adventure, knowing that she was part of a greater plan and that her efforts, no matter how small, made a difference.

Hannah's story became an inspiration to many, a testament to the power of faith, resilience, and the transformative impact of love and service. She had set out on her missionary journey with a heart full of hope and a desire to make a difference, and she had discovered that the true reward lay in the connections she had made and the lives she had touched.

And so, the young missionary's journey continued, guided by faith and driven by a deep sense of calling. Hannah Stevens had found her purpose in serving others, and her story was a beacon of hope, reminding all who heard it that even in the most remote and challenging places, the light of Christ's love could shine brightly.

Chapter 10: A Child's Prayer

The quaint town of Harmony Ridge was a close-knit community where everyone knew each other, and the local church stood at the center of their lives. Nestled among rolling hills and lush green fields, the town was a picturesque haven of peace and simplicity. St. Matthew's Church, with its tall steeple and stained-glass windows, was not just a place of worship but a gathering place for the entire town.

Among the parishioners of St. Matthew's was the Thompson family. John and Sarah Thompson were devoted members of the church, and their seven-year-old daughter, Lily, was the light of their lives. Lily was a bright and cheerful child, known for her boundless energy and innocent faith. She loved attending Sunday school, where she eagerly absorbed Bible stories and sang hymns with enthusiasm.

One summer, Harmony Ridge faced a severe drought. The usually lush fields turned brown and brittle, the streams dried up, and the townspeople grew increasingly anxious about their crops and livestock. The town had always relied on agriculture, and the drought threatened their livelihoods. Despite their prayers and efforts, there seemed to be no relief in sight.

As the weeks passed, the situation grew dire. The congregation of St. Matthew's gathered for special prayer services, pleading for rain to save their town. Each service was filled with heartfelt prayers and hymns, but the skies remained stubbornly clear. The once hopeful community began to lose faith, their spirits dampened by the relentless heat and parched earth.

Lily, however, remained steadfast in her belief that God would answer their prayers. Her innocent faith was unwavering, and she often reminded her parents and friends that God was listening and that they just needed to keep praying. Her words brought comfort to those around her, but many still struggled to believe that a miracle was possible.

One Sunday morning, as the congregation gathered for another prayer service, Lily felt a strong urge to do something more. She had been thinking about the story of Elijah and the prophets of Baal, where Elijah's faith had brought down fire from heaven. Inspired by this story, she decided to write a letter to God, asking for rain.

After the service, Lily sat down at the kitchen table with a piece of paper and a crayon. She carefully wrote out her prayer, pouring her heart into every word:

"Dear God,

We really need rain in Harmony Ridge. Our crops are dying, and the animals are thirsty. I know You can make it rain because You love us and want to help us. Please send rain soon.

Love, Lily"

Lily folded the letter and placed it in an envelope. She addressed it simply to "God" and drew a small heart on the front. She then asked her parents if they could help her mail the letter.

John and Sarah were touched by Lily's faith and determination. Though they knew the letter wouldn't actually reach God through the mail, they didn't want to dampen her spirit. Instead, they decided to take the letter to Pastor David and ask him to include it in the next prayer service.

That evening, the Thompson family visited Pastor David at his home. Lily handed him the envelope, her eyes shining with hope. "Pastor David, can you please read this letter during the next service? It's a prayer for rain."

Pastor David smiled warmly and took the envelope. "Of course, Lily. I will make sure to read it. Thank you for your faith and your beautiful prayer."

The following Sunday, the church was filled with the usual congregation, their faces reflecting the weariness and worry of the ongoing drought. Pastor David began the service with a prayer, asking for God's mercy and intervention. Then he held up the envelope and explained to the congregation that Lily had written a special letter to God.

"Lily has written a heartfelt prayer, asking for rain to save our town. I believe her innocent faith can touch all of us and remind us of the power of prayer."

Pastor David opened the envelope and read Lily's letter aloud. The simple, sincere words moved the congregation deeply. Tears filled many eyes as they listened to the child's plea for help. The letter was a reminder of the pure and unwavering faith that often gets lost in the complexities of adult life.

After reading the letter, Pastor David led the congregation in a unified prayer, echoing Lily's words and asking God to send rain. The church was filled with a powerful sense of hope and togetherness, as everyone joined in the prayer with renewed faith.

As the service concluded, the congregation filed out of the church, feeling a sense of peace and optimism they hadn't felt in weeks. They shared smiles and words of encouragement, grateful for the reminder of the power of faith.

That night, as Lily lay in bed, she whispered another prayer, thanking God for listening and asking once more for rain. She fell asleep with a sense of calm, trusting that God would answer in His own time.

The next day, the sky remained clear and the heat continued, but the mood in Harmony Ridge was different. The townspeople went about their work with a renewed sense of hope, buoyed by Lily's faith and the unity of their prayer.

Two days later, as the sun began to set, dark clouds started to gather on the horizon. The air grew cooler, and a gentle breeze rustled the leaves. The townspeople watched the sky with bated breath, unsure if the clouds would bring the much-needed rain.

Lily was playing in the yard when she noticed the clouds. She ran inside, calling out to her parents. "Mom, Dad! Look at the sky! I think it's going to rain!"

John and Sarah joined her outside, their hearts pounding with anticipation. They watched as the clouds grew darker and more ominous, and the first drops of rain began to fall. What started as a gentle drizzle quickly turned into a steady downpour, soaking the parched earth and filling the air with the sweet scent of rain.

The townspeople rejoiced, running outside to feel the rain on their skin and to give thanks for the answered prayers. Farmers knelt in their fields, tears of gratitude mingling with the raindrops. Children splashed in puddles, their laughter echoing through the streets.

The rain continued through the night, replenishing the dry streams and nourishing the thirsty crops. By morning, the town was transformed, the fields green and vibrant once more. The drought was broken, and hope was restored.

The following Sunday, St. Matthew's Church was filled with a joyful congregation. Pastor David stood before them, his heart full of gratitude and awe. "God has heard our prayers and sent the rain we so desperately needed. Let us give thanks for His mercy and for the faith that brought us together."

He then called Lily to the front of the church, her face glowing with happiness. "Lily's innocent faith and her heartfelt prayer touched us all and reminded us of the power of believing. Thank you, Lily, for showing us the way."

The congregation erupted in applause, their hearts full of love and admiration for the young girl who had inspired them all. Lily smiled shyly, feeling the warmth and support of her community.

After the service, many people came up to thank Lily and share how her prayer had renewed their own faith. One elderly woman, Mrs. Johnson, took Lily's hands in hers and said, "Your faith has been a blessing to us all, dear. Never lose that beautiful belief in God's love."

As the weeks passed, the rain continued to fall at regular intervals, ensuring a bountiful harvest and replenishing the town's water sources. The people of Harmony Ridge were filled with gratitude, and their faith was stronger than ever.

Lily's prayer and the subsequent rain became a cherished story in Harmony Ridge, a testament to the power of innocent faith and the miracles that can happen when a community comes together in prayer. The story was told and retold, becoming a part of the town's legacy.

For Lily, the experience was a profound lesson in the power of faith and the importance of trusting in God's plan. She continued to grow in her faith, always remembering the day her prayer was answered and the rain came to Harmony Ridge.

Years later, as an adult, Lily often reflected on that summer and the impact it had on her life. She became an active member of her church, leading Sunday school and sharing her story with the next generation. She wanted to inspire others to hold on to their faith and to believe in the power of prayer.

One Sunday, as she was teaching a group of young children, she told them the story of the drought and her prayer for rain. The children listened with wide eyes, captivated by the tale of faith and miracles.

"Remember," Lily told them, "God hears all our prayers, no matter how small. And sometimes, it's the faith of a child that can move mountains and bring about the most surprising turn of events."

The children nodded, their hearts touched by the story. They left the class with a sense of wonder and belief, their own faith strengthened by Lily's words.

As Lily walked home that evening, she looked up at the sky, remembering the dark clouds that had brought rain to her town all those years ago. She felt a deep sense of gratitude for the journey of faith she had walked and for the blessings that had come from a simple child's prayer.

The story of Lily's prayer continued to be a source of inspiration for the people of Harmony Ridge. It was a reminder that faith, no matter how small, can bring about great change and that the innocent belief of a child can touch the hearts of an entire community.

And so, the legacy of that summer lived on, a testament to the power of faith, the strength of community, and the miracles that can happen when we trust in God's love.

Chapter 11: The Christmas Miracle

The small town of Evergreen nestled in the heart of New England was renowned for its picturesque winters. As the first snowflakes of December began to fall, the town transformed into a winter wonderland, with twinkling lights adorning every street and evergreen wreaths hanging from every door. Christmas in Evergreen was a magical time, but this year, a sense of unease lingered in the air.

The economic downturn had hit Evergreen hard. Many families were struggling to make ends meet, and the usual festive cheer was overshadowed by worries about bills and job security. The town's annual Christmas celebration, a tradition that had brought joy to generations, was at risk of being canceled due to a lack of funds.

Emma Bennett, the owner of the town's bakery, felt the weight of the season's hardships more than most. Her bakery, Emma's Sweet Delights, had been a cornerstone of the community for years. Emma was known for her kindness, her delicious treats, and her unwavering holiday spirit. But this year, even her optimism was tested.

As she kneaded dough one frosty morning, Emma's thoughts drifted to the families in Evergreen who might not have gifts under the tree or a Christmas dinner to share. She knew she had to do something to help, but she wasn't sure where to start.

The bell above the bakery door jingled, snapping Emma out of her reverie. She looked up to see Pastor John, the beloved pastor of Evergreen Community Church, walking in with a warm smile.

"Good morning, Emma," Pastor John greeted her. "I hope I'm not interrupting."

"Not at all, Pastor John," Emma replied, wiping her hands on her apron. "What brings you by?"

"I've been thinking about our community and how we can make this Christmas special, despite the challenges we're facing," Pastor John said, taking a seat at one of the bakery's cozy tables. "I know it's a difficult time for many, but I believe that if we come together, we can create a Christmas miracle."

Emma's eyes lit up with a glimmer of hope. "What do you have in mind?"

Pastor John leaned forward, his expression earnest. "I propose we organize a community-wide Christmas event. We can collect donations, gather volunteers, and create a celebration that brings joy and hope to everyone in Evergreen. I know it won't be easy, but with God's guidance and the support of our community, I believe we can make it happen."

Emma felt a surge of inspiration. "I love the idea, Pastor John. Count me in. I'll do whatever I can to help."

"Thank you, Emma," Pastor John said, his smile widening. "Your enthusiasm is exactly what we need. I'll start reaching out to other community members, and we can hold a planning meeting at the church this evening. Are you available?"

"I'll be there," Emma replied, feeling a renewed sense of purpose.

That evening, a small but dedicated group of townspeople gathered in the church's fellowship hall. There was Pastor John, Emma, Mr. Thompson, the town's retired school principal, Mrs. Harris, the librarian, and several other community leaders. They discussed their ideas and brainstormed ways to bring the Christmas celebration to life.

"We'll need donations of food, gifts, and decorations," Pastor John said. "And we'll need volunteers to help set up and organize the event. Any suggestions on how we can make this happen?"

Emma raised her hand. "I can bake treats and provide hot cocoa. We can set up a booth in the town square to collect donations and spread the word about the event."

Mrs. Harris chimed in, "I can organize a book drive for the children. We'll gather gently used books and wrap them as gifts."

Mr. Thompson added, "I'll talk to the school about having the students create decorations and handmade cards. It will be a wonderful way for them to get involved."

As ideas flowed and plans took shape, the sense of camaraderie in the room grew. Everyone was determined to make the Christmas celebration a success, despite the challenges they faced.

In the days that followed, the spirit of giving spread throughout Evergreen. The bakery became a hub of activity as Emma and her volunteers baked cookies, cakes, and pies. The aroma of cinnamon and gingerbread filled the air, drawing people in and lifting their spirits. Donations poured in from local businesses and residents, filling the collection booths with toys, food, and warm clothing.

The town square, usually quiet during the winter months, buzzed with excitement as volunteers decorated trees, hung lights, and set up booths. The schoolchildren crafted beautiful ornaments and cards, their laughter and creativity adding to the festive atmosphere.

As the day of the event approached, the weather forecast predicted a heavy snowfall. Many worried that the snow would hinder the celebration, but Emma remained hopeful. "A little snow won't stop us," she said with determination. "In fact, it might make our Christmas celebration even more magical."

On the morning of the event, the town square was transformed into a winter wonderland. Fresh snow blanketed the ground, sparkling under the twinkling lights. The scent of pine mingled with the sweet aroma of baked goods, and cheerful music filled the air.

Families began to arrive, bundled up in coats and scarves, their faces alight with anticipation. The sight of children laughing and playing in the snow, their eyes wide with wonder, warmed Emma's heart. She knew that this celebration would bring joy to many, even if just for a day.

The event kicked off with a heartfelt speech from Pastor John, who thanked everyone for their generosity and reminded them of the true spirit of Christmas. "Christmas is a time of giving, of coming together to share love and hope," he said. "Today, we are not just celebrating the season, but the strength and unity of our community."

The festivities began in earnest, with activities for all ages. There were booths offering hot cocoa, freshly baked treats, and savory foods. Children lined up to receive gifts from Santa Claus, played by Mr. Thompson, whose jolly demeanor and hearty laugh brought smiles to their faces.

Mrs. Harris's book drive was a hit, with children excitedly unwrapping their new books and settling down to read by the warmth of a crackling fire pit.

The handmade ornaments and cards created by the schoolchildren adorned the trees and brought a personal touch to the decorations.

Emma was busy at the bakery booth, serving up her famous gingerbread cookies and hot apple cider. She couldn't help but feel a deep sense of gratitude for the way the community had come together. Despite the hardships they faced, they had created something beautiful and meaningful.

As the day turned to evening, the town square glowed with the soft light of lanterns and Christmas lights. The air was filled with the sound of carolers singing beloved holiday songs, their voices harmonizing in perfect unity.

Then, just as the celebration seemed to be winding down, a surprising turn of events unfolded. A group of townspeople who had moved away over the years returned to Evergreen, bringing with them donations and heartfelt messages of support. They had heard about the community's efforts and wanted to contribute to the Christmas miracle.

Among them was David, Emma's childhood friend, who had moved to the city for work. He approached Emma with a smile, holding a large box filled with toys and supplies. "I heard about what you all were doing and knew I had to come back to help," he said. "Evergreen has always been home, and it's heartwarming to see the community coming together like this."

Emma's eyes welled with tears of joy. "Thank you, David. This means so much to all of us. It's a reminder that no matter where we go, the spirit of Evergreen lives in our hearts."

The unexpected arrival of old friends and neighbors added a new layer of warmth to the celebration. It was a testament to the enduring bonds of community and the power of coming together in times of need.

As the night drew to a close, Pastor John gathered everyone around the large Christmas tree in the center of the square. He led them in a final prayer, thanking God for the blessings of the day and for the strength and unity of their community.

"Dear Lord, we thank You for this beautiful day and for the love and generosity that have brought us together. We are grateful for the miracles, both big and small, that remind us of Your presence in our lives. As we celebrate this Christmas season, may we continue to share Your love and hope with those around us. Amen."

The crowd echoed the "Amen," their hearts filled with gratitude and joy. The Christmas celebration had been a resounding success, a true testament to the spirit of the season and the power of community.

In the weeks that followed, the town of Evergreen continued to feel the positive impact of their Christmas miracle. The event had not only brought joy and hope to those in need but had also strengthened the bonds within the community. People reached out to support one another, offering help and kindness in ways big and small.

Emma reflected on the experience, feeling a deep sense of fulfillment. She knew that the true spirit of Christmas was not found in material gifts or grand gestures, but in the simple acts of love and compassion that touched the hearts of those around her.

One evening, as she sat by the fire in her cozy home, Emma received a letter from David. He had returned to the city but wanted to share his thoughts about the Christmas celebration and the impact it had on him.

"Dear Emma,

I wanted to thank you again for the incredible Christmas celebration in Evergreen. It was a reminder of what truly matters in life—love, community, and the spirit of giving. Being back in Evergreen and seeing the way everyone came together was a gift in itself.

I've been inspired by what we accomplished and have decided to start a similar initiative in my city. I want to bring that same sense of hope and unity to others who are struggling. Your leadership and kindness have been a beacon of light, and I'm grateful to call you my friend.

Wishing you all the best,

David"

Emma smiled as she read the letter, feeling a sense of pride and joy. The Christmas miracle in Evergreen had not only touched their town but had also inspired others to spread the same message of love and hope.

As the years went by, the memory of that special Christmas continued to be a cherished story in Evergreen. It was a reminder of the power of faith, the strength of community, and the true meaning of the season. The Christmas miracle had brought joy and hope to those in need, and its impact would be felt for generations to come.

And so, the town of Evergreen continued to thrive, its heart filled with the spirit of Christmas all year round. The legacy of that miraculous day lived on, a testament to the enduring power of love and the miracles that happen when a community comes together in faith and compassion.

Chapter 12: The Test of Faith

Mark Peterson had always been a man of strong faith. Raised in a devout Christian family in the heart of the Midwest, he grew up attending church every Sunday, participating in Bible study groups, and volunteering for community service. His faith had been a guiding light through life's ups and downs, providing him with a sense of purpose and strength.

Mark's life was, by all appearances, blessed. He had a loving wife, Rachel, and two wonderful children, Emily and Joshua. He worked as an engineer at a reputable firm and was respected in his community for his integrity and kindness. Mark and Rachel were actively involved in their church, St. Luke's, where they were known for their generosity and willingness to help others.

However, life has a way of testing even the strongest faith, and Mark's was about to be tested in ways he could never have imagined.

It was a sunny Saturday afternoon in early summer. Mark and his family were enjoying a picnic at a nearby park, a tradition they cherished. The children played Frisbee on the lush green lawn while Mark and Rachel sat on a blanket, savoring the simple pleasure of being together.

Suddenly, Mark's phone rang, interrupting the peaceful scene. He glanced at the caller ID and saw that it was his mother. "I wonder what she needs," he said, more to himself than to Rachel.

"Go ahead and answer," Rachel encouraged. "It might be important."

Mark picked up the call, expecting to hear his mother's familiar, warm voice. Instead, he was met with the frantic, tearful voice of his sister, Lisa.

"Mark, you need to come to the hospital right away. It's Dad. He's had a heart attack."

Mark's world tilted on its axis. His father, a robust and active man in his early seventies, had always been the picture of health. The idea of him suffering a heart attack was unthinkable. "We'll be there as soon as we can," he managed to say, his voice shaking.

Rachel looked at him with concern as he ended the call. "What's wrong?"

"It's Dad," Mark said, struggling to keep his composure. "He's had a heart attack. We need to go to the hospital."

They quickly gathered their things and hurried to the car, the children's laughter fading as the gravity of the situation became apparent. The drive to the hospital was a blur of fear and prayers. Mark clung to his faith, repeating over and over in his mind, "God, please let him be okay. Please."

When they arrived at the hospital, they found Lisa in the waiting room, her face pale and streaked with tears. She rushed to Mark and embraced him tightly. "He's in surgery now. The doctors are doing everything they can."

Mark nodded, his heart pounding. "Have you talked to Mom?"

"She's on her way," Lisa replied. "She's coming as fast as she can."

They sat in the waiting room, the minutes stretching into an agonizing eternity. Mark held Rachel's hand tightly, drawing strength from her presence. They prayed together, their whispered words a lifeline in the storm of uncertainty.

Finally, the surgeon emerged, his expression grave. "Mr. Peterson's condition is critical. We've done all we can, but the next 24 hours will be crucial. We're monitoring him closely, but you should prepare for the possibility that he might not make it."

The words hit Mark like a sledgehammer. He felt a wave of disbelief, followed by a surge of anger and fear. How could this be happening? His father was supposed to be invincible. The pillar of their family.

"Can we see him?" Lisa asked, her voice trembling.

"Yes, but only for a few minutes," the surgeon said. "He's in the ICU. Please follow me."

Mark and Lisa followed the surgeon down the sterile, fluorescent-lit hallway to the intensive care unit. There, lying motionless on a bed, surrounded by beeping machines and tubes, was their father. The sight was almost too much to bear.

Mark approached the bed, his heart breaking at the sight of his father so vulnerable and frail. He reached out and gently took his father's hand. "Dad, it's Mark. We're here. We're praying for you."

Tears streamed down Lisa's face as she stood on the other side of the bed, holding their father's other hand. "We love you, Dad. Please hang on."

The next hours were a blur of waiting and praying. Family members and friends arrived, offering support and sharing in the vigil. Mark's mother, Carol, arrived and collapsed into his arms, her sobs wracking her body. Mark held her tightly, whispering reassurances that felt hollow even as he spoke them.

As the night wore on, Mark found himself alone in the hospital chapel. He knelt at the altar, his heart heavy with anguish. "God, I don't understand why this is happening. Please, please save my father. He's a good man. We need him."

In the silence of the chapel, Mark felt a sense of peace wash over him, a reminder of God's presence even in the darkest of times. He clung to that feeling, drawing strength from his faith.

The next morning, the family received a glimmer of hope. The doctors reported that Mark's father's condition had stabilized slightly. He was still critical, but there was a chance he might pull through. Mark felt a surge of relief and gratitude. "Thank you, God," he whispered. "Thank you."

The following weeks were a rollercoaster of emotions. Mark's father slowly improved, though the road to recovery was long and uncertain. Mark spent as much time as he could at the hospital, balancing work, family, and his father's care. His faith was his anchor, but the strain was immense.

One evening, as Mark sat by his father's bedside, his father opened his eyes and looked at him. "Mark," he whispered, his voice weak but steady.

"Dad," Mark said, his heart leaping with joy. "You're awake."

His father managed a faint smile. "Thank you for being here. Thank you for your prayers."

Tears filled Mark's eyes. "I would do anything for you, Dad. I love you."

"I love you too, son," his father replied. "God has been with me through this. I felt His presence, even when I was unconscious. He is always with us."

Mark nodded, his heart swelling with gratitude. His father's faith was unshaken, even in the face of death. It was a powerful reminder of the strength that came from believing in God's presence.

As his father continued to recover, Mark felt his own faith deepen. He realized that his father's illness, though devastating, had brought him closer to God. He had learned to trust in God's plan, even when it was difficult to understand.

Months later, Mark's father was well enough to return home. The family gathered to celebrate his recovery, their hearts filled with gratitude and joy. They knew that the journey was far from over, but they faced it together, their faith stronger than ever.

One Sunday, as they sat in church, Pastor Williams delivered a sermon about the testing of faith. He spoke about the trials that everyone faces and how those trials can strengthen one's relationship with God.

"Faith is not about having all the answers," Pastor Williams said. "It's about trusting in God, even when we don't understand His plan. It's about knowing that He is with us, no matter what we face."

Mark listened intently, his heart resonating with the message. He had experienced the truth of those words firsthand. His faith had been tested, and through that test, he had found a deeper understanding of God's presence in his life.

After the service, Pastor Williams approached Mark and his family. "Mark, I've been praying for you and your family. I'm so glad to see your father here today."

"Thank you, Pastor," Mark said. "It's been a difficult journey, but we've felt God's presence every step of the way."

"Faith is often tested in ways we can't anticipate," Pastor Williams said. "But through those tests, we grow stronger. Your family's faith has been an inspiration to all of us."

Mark felt a surge of gratitude for the support of his church community. Their prayers and encouragement had been a source of strength during the darkest times.

As the weeks turned into months, life gradually returned to normal. Mark's father continued to improve, and the family settled back into their routines. But the experience had left an indelible mark on Mark's soul. He had learned to see God's hand in every aspect of his life, even in the trials and challenges.

One evening, as Mark and Rachel sat on the porch, watching the sunset, Rachel turned to him and said, "Mark, I'm so proud of how you've handled everything. Your faith has been a rock for all of us."

Mark smiled, his heart filled with love for his wife. "I couldn't have done it without you, Rachel. You've been my strength and my support."

"We've been each other's strength," Rachel said, taking his hand. "And our faith has carried us through."

As they watched the sun dip below the horizon, Mark felt a deep sense of peace. He knew that there would be more tests of faith in the future, but he was ready to face them with the strength and understanding he had gained.

One particular test came a few months later when Mark received unexpected news from his company. Due to budget cuts and restructuring, his position was being eliminated. The news hit him hard, stirring a mix of emotions—fear, frustration, and uncertainty. Losing his job felt like another blow, just when he thought life was stabilizing.

He broke the news to Rachel that evening, trying to mask his worry. "Rachel, I've got some bad news. The company is downsizing, and my position has been cut. I'm out of a job."

RACHEL'S EYES WIDENED in surprise, but she quickly embraced him. "We'll get through this, Mark. We've faced bigger challenges before, and we've come out stronger. This will be no different."

Her unwavering support and optimism reassured him, but the fear of the unknown lingered. That night, as he lay in bed, Mark prayed fervently, asking God for guidance and strength. "Lord, I trust in You. Help me to see the path You have laid out for me."

The next morning, Mark began his job search in earnest. He updated his resume, reached out to contacts, and applied for numerous positions. Despite the initial anxiety, he felt a sense of calm knowing that God had a plan for him.

Days turned into weeks, and the search continued. Mark faced rejections and setbacks, but he remained hopeful. He spent more time in prayer and reflection, seeking to understand what God was teaching him through this trial.

One afternoon, as he was going through job listings, Mark received a call from a former colleague, Sarah, who had started her own engineering consultancy firm. "Mark, I heard about your situation. I have an opening at my firm, and I think you'd be a perfect fit. Are you interested?"

Mark felt a surge of hope. "Thank you, Sarah. I'd love to learn more about the position."

They arranged a meeting, and within a week, Mark had a new job. The position not only matched his skills and experience but also offered opportunities for growth and a better work-life balance.

As he shared the news with Rachel, she hugged him tightly. "I knew something good would come out of this. God always provides."

Mark felt a deep sense of gratitude. The experience had reinforced his belief in God's faithfulness and timing. He realized that losing his job had been a test of faith, one that had ultimately led him to a better place.

Months later, as Mark reflected on his journey, he saw how each trial had deepened his faith and brought him closer to God. He understood that faith was not about avoiding challenges but about trusting God through them.

During a church service, Mark felt moved to share his testimony. Standing before the congregation, he spoke about the trials he had faced—the heart attack that had almost taken his father, the job loss, and the uncertainty that had tested his faith.

"Through each challenge," Mark said, "I've learned to see God's hand at work. I've learned that faith is about trusting Him, even when we don't understand His plan. God has been with me every step of the way, and His presence has brought me strength and peace."

The congregation listened intently, moved by Mark's words. His testimony resonated with many who had faced their own trials and found strength in their faith.

After the service, Pastor Williams approached Mark with a smile. "Thank you for sharing your story, Mark. Your journey is a powerful reminder of God's faithfulness. It's a testament to the strength that comes from trusting in Him."

Mark felt a deep sense of fulfillment. Sharing his story had not only reinforced his own faith but had also inspired others. He knew that life would continue to bring challenges, but he was ready to face them with the understanding and strength he had gained.

As he walked out of the church, surrounded by the support and love of his community, Mark felt a renewed sense of purpose. His faith had been tested, but through those tests, he had found a deeper connection to God.

In the years that followed, Mark continued to grow in his faith. He remained active in his church, helping others who faced their own trials and sharing the lessons he had learned. His journey had taught him that faith was not about having all the answers but about trusting God through the uncertainties of life.

One evening, as Mark and Rachel sat together, watching another beautiful sunset, Mark took Rachel's hand and said, "We've been through so much, Rachel. But through it all, our faith has grown stronger. I'm grateful for every trial because it has brought us closer to God and to each other."

Rachel smiled, her eyes reflecting the love and understanding that had deepened over the years. "I wouldn't change a thing, Mark. Every challenge has been a blessing in disguise, and our faith has been our anchor."

As they sat in peaceful silence, Mark felt a profound sense of gratitude. He knew that life would continue to bring its tests, but he also knew that with faith, he could face anything. His journey had been a testament to the power of faith, the strength of community, and the unwavering presence of God in his life.

And so, Mark Peterson's story was a powerful reminder that faith, when tested, can lead to a deeper understanding of God's love and presence. It was a journey of trials and triumphs, of challenges and growth, and of a faith that had been strengthened and refined through the fire.

Chapter 13: Grace Under Fire

The year was 2003, and the world was a place of turmoil. The war in Iraq had begun, and soldiers from around the globe were called to serve. Among them was Captain Jonathan Brooks, a dedicated and devout Christian who had enlisted in the army straight out of college. His faith had always been a cornerstone of his life, guiding him through every challenge he faced. Now, as he prepared to enter the horrors of war, he leaned on that faith more than ever.

Jonathan, known as "Captain Brooks" to his comrades, was respected for his leadership and compassion. He had a quiet strength about him, a calm in the storm that inspired those around him. He often carried a small, worn Bible in his breast pocket, a gift from his mother before he left for boot camp. The pages were dog-eared and highlighted, filled with notes and prayers that had seen him through countless nights.

The deployment to Iraq was Jonathan's first combat mission. He and his unit were stationed in a remote outpost near Fallujah, tasked with maintaining peace and order in a region rife with conflict. The days were long and grueling, filled with the constant threat of danger. The soldiers faced ambushes, roadside bombs, and sniper fire, all while trying to build trust with the local population.

From the moment they arrived, it was clear that this would be unlike anything they had ever experienced. The searing heat, the pervasive dust, and the constant noise of warfare created a relentless tension that wore on everyone. Yet, in the midst of it all, Jonathan remained a beacon of hope and strength for his men.

One evening, as the sun dipped below the horizon, casting a fiery glow over the desert, Jonathan gathered his men for a moment of reflection. They sat in a circle, their faces grim and weary, the weight of the day's events heavy on their shoulders.

"Gentlemen," Jonathan began, his voice steady but filled with compassion, "I know these are difficult times. We are far from home, facing dangers we never imagined. But I want you to remember that we are not alone. God is with us, even here, even now."

He pulled out his Bible and read from Psalm 23: "The Lord is my shepherd; I shall not want. He maketh me to lie down in green pastures: he leadeth me beside the still waters. He restoreth my soul: he leadeth me in the paths of righteousness for his name's sake. Yea, though I walk through the valley of the shadow of death, I will fear no evil: for thou art with me; thy rod and thy staff they comfort me."

The familiar words brought a sense of peace to the soldiers, a reminder of the faith that sustained them. They bowed their heads in prayer, seeking comfort and strength from a higher power. For Jonathan, these moments of fellowship were a lifeline, a way to reaffirm his own faith and to provide solace to his comrades.

The following weeks were marked by a series of intense and harrowing encounters. Jonathan's unit was involved in several firefights, each one leaving a mark on their spirits. The soldiers grew closer, their bond forged in the crucible of combat. Jonathan was a steady presence, his faith a guiding light in the darkness.

One particularly brutal day, the unit was ambushed while on patrol. The enemy's gunfire was relentless, and the soldiers were pinned down, their situation growing increasingly desperate. Jonathan rallied his men, organizing a defensive position and calling for reinforcements. Amidst the chaos, he found a moment to pray, asking for God's protection and guidance.

The battle raged for hours, but finally, the reinforcements arrived, and the enemy was driven back. The cost, however, was high. Several of Jonathan's men were wounded, and one, Private First Class Michael Jenkins, was critically injured.

As the medics worked to stabilize Michael, Jonathan knelt beside him, holding his hand. "Stay with us, Michael," he whispered, his voice choked with emotion. "You're not alone. We're here, and God is with you."

Michael's eyes fluttered open, his face pale and etched with pain. "Captain," he murmured, "I'm scared."

"I know, Michael," Jonathan replied, his grip tightening. "But I want you to hold on to your faith. God is with you, and He will see you through this. Let me pray for you."

Jonathan prayed fervently, his words a plea for healing and strength. The other soldiers gathered around, their heads bowed in solidarity. The bond they shared, strengthened by their faith, provided a source of comfort and hope.

Despite the best efforts of the medics, Michael's condition worsened. He was airlifted to a field hospital, but the prognosis was grim. The news hit the unit hard, a stark reminder of the fragility of life in a war zone.

Jonathan struggled with the loss, his heart heavy with grief. He spent long hours in prayer, seeking solace and understanding. He knew that his faith was being tested, but he also knew that he had to remain strong for his men.

One night, as he sat alone in his tent, Jonathan opened his Bible to the Book of Job. The story of Job's suffering and unwavering faith resonated deeply with him. He read the passages slowly, absorbing the words and drawing strength from them.

"Though he slay me, yet will I trust in him," Jonathan read aloud, his voice steady. "I will maintain mine own ways before him. He also shall be my salvation."

The words brought a sense of clarity and peace. Jonathan realized that his faith was not about having all the answers but about trusting in God's plan, even in the face of unimaginable hardship. He felt a renewed sense of purpose, a determination to continue his mission and to be a source of strength for his men.

The next day, Jonathan gathered his unit for a meeting. He spoke to them about Michael, about the pain of loss, and about the importance of holding on to their faith.

"We have faced great trials, and we will face more in the days ahead," Jonathan said, his voice filled with conviction. "But we must remember that we are not alone. God is with us, and our faith will sustain us. We must honor Michael's memory by continuing to fight with courage and integrity."

The soldiers nodded, their faces reflecting a mix of grief and resolve. They knew that the road ahead would be difficult, but they also knew that they had each other and that their faith would guide them.

As the weeks turned into months, the unit continued their mission, facing new challenges and dangers. Jonathan remained a steadfast leader, his faith a constant source of strength. He saw the impact of his example on his men, their own faith deepening as they navigated the horrors of war.

One evening, as they returned to their outpost after a successful mission, Jonathan gathered his men for a moment of reflection. They sat around a campfire, the flickering flames casting shadows on their weary faces.

"Gentlemen," Jonathan began, "we have been through a lot together. We have faced fear, loss, and uncertainty. But through it all, we have held on to our faith. And it is that faith that has given us the strength to keep going."

He looked around at the faces of his comrades, men he had come to regard as brothers. "I want you to know how proud I am of each and every one of you. Your courage, your resilience, and your faith have inspired me. We have been tested, but we have come through stronger. And I believe that God has a plan for each of us, even in this war-torn land."

The soldiers nodded, their expressions reflecting a mix of gratitude and determination. They knew that their journey was far from over, but they also knew that they had the strength to face whatever lay ahead.

As they bowed their heads in prayer, Jonathan felt a deep sense of peace. He knew that his faith had been tested in ways he could never have imagined, but he also knew that it had grown stronger. He had found a deeper understanding of God's presence in his life, a presence that had guided him through the darkest of times.

The next day, the unit received orders for a new mission, one that would take them deep into enemy territory. It was a daunting task, but Jonathan and his men were ready. They had faced countless challenges before, and they would face this one with the same courage and faith.

As they prepared to leave, Jonathan took a moment to read from his Bible, sharing a passage with his men. "Have I not commanded you? Be strong and courageous. Do not be afraid; do not be discouraged, for the Lord your God will be with you wherever you go."

The words resonated deeply with the soldiers, a reminder of the strength and guidance that came from their faith. They set out on their mission with a sense of purpose and determination, knowing that they were not alone.

The mission was one of the most challenging they had faced. They encountered fierce resistance, and the danger was constant. But through it all, Jonathan's leadership and faith provided a steady anchor for his men. They fought with courage and integrity, drawing strength from their bond and their belief in a higher power.

As they completed their mission and returned to their outpost, the soldiers felt a sense of accomplishment and relief. They had faced the fire and emerged stronger, their faith intact.

In the days that followed, Jonathan reflected on his journey. He had faced unimaginable horrors and had been tested in ways he never thought possible. But through it all, his faith had been his guide, providing comfort and strength.

He realized that his role as a leader was not just about tactics and strategy but about being a source of hope and inspiration. He had seen the impact of his faith on his men, how it had given them the courage to face each day. And he knew that he had been called to this mission for a reason.

One evening, as the sun set over the desert, casting a golden glow over the landscape, Jonathan sat alone, his Bible in his hands. He opened it to a passage that had brought him comfort many times before: "The Lord is my light and my salvation—whom shall I fear? The Lord is the stronghold of my life—of whom shall I be afraid?"

The words brought a sense of peace and clarity. Jonathan knew that he was exactly where he was meant to be, doing exactly what he was meant to do. His faith had been tested, and it had not wavered. He had found grace under fire, a deeper understanding of God's presence in his life.

As he closed his Bible and looked out at the vast, silent desert, Jonathan felt a profound sense of gratitude. He knew that the road ahead would be difficult, but he also knew that he had the strength to face it. His faith would continue to guide him, providing comfort and strength to his comrades and himself.

The war continued, but so did the bonds of brotherhood and faith that Jonathan had fostered within his unit. Each soldier carried a piece of that faith with them, a light in the darkness, a reminder that they were never alone.

Years later, as Jonathan looked back on his time in Iraq, he saw it not as a period of suffering and hardship but as a journey of growth and understanding. His faith had been tested, and it had emerged stronger. He had found grace under fire, and that grace had guided him through the darkest of times.

Jonathan's story was a testament to the power of faith, the strength of community, and the unwavering presence of God in the most challenging circumstances. It was a reminder that, even in the midst of war, there is hope, there is love, and there is grace.

Chapter 14: The Samaritan's Kindness

I. The Start of a New Day

The early morning sunlight filtered through the sheer curtains of Emma Thompson's cozy apartment, casting a warm, golden hue across the room. Emma, a 32-year-old school teacher, was already up, preparing for another day of teaching at the local high school. Her routine was simple but comforting: a cup of freshly brewed coffee, a quick glance at the newspaper, and a quiet moment of reflection.

Emma had always been a woman of faith, deeply committed to her Christian values. Her days were often filled with the hustle and bustle of teaching, but she made it a point to start each day with a prayer, seeking guidance and strength for the tasks ahead.

As she sipped her coffee, Emma glanced at the clock and realized she had just enough time to stop by the local bakery to pick up some treats for her students. She quickly got dressed, grabbed her purse, and headed out the door. The cool morning air was invigorating, and Emma felt a sense of anticipation for the day ahead.

The bakery was a charming little shop nestled on the corner of Main Street. Emma entered, greeted by the warm aroma of freshly baked goods. She smiled at the baker, Mrs. Johnson, who was busy arranging pastries behind the counter.

"Good morning, Mrs. Johnson! I'm here to pick up a dozen muffins for my class," Emma said cheerfully.

"Good morning, Emma!" Mrs. Johnson replied with a smile. "I've got just the thing for you. I'll have them ready in a few minutes."

Emma waited as Mrs. Johnson prepared the muffins. She took the opportunity to chat with a few regular customers and enjoy the lively atmosphere of the bakery. It was a small, comforting ritual that helped her feel connected to her community.

As Emma was about to leave the bakery, her phone buzzed with a notification. She glanced at it and saw a news alert about a car accident on a nearby road. The details were scarce, but it mentioned multiple injuries and emergency responders at the scene.

A sudden impulse to check on the situation seized Emma. She made a quick decision to drive by the accident site before heading to school. She knew it might be an inconvenience, but her instinct to help was stronger than her desire to stick to her routine.

II. The Scene of the Accident

EMMA DROVE TOWARD THE accident site, her heart racing with concern. The road was congested with emergency vehicles and bystanders, creating a chaotic scene. Emma parked her car at a safe distance and approached the area on foot.

The accident had been severe. Two cars were involved, one of them a minivan with a crumpled front end. Paramedics were attending to several injured people, and the air was filled with the sounds of sirens and muffled conversations.

Emma's eyes scanned the scene, searching for anyone who might need immediate assistance. She noticed a young woman sitting on the curb, her face pale and her hands trembling. She appeared to be in shock, and Emma instinctively approached her.

"Hi, I'm Emma," she said gently, sitting down beside the woman. "Are you okay? Can I help you with anything?"

The woman looked at Emma, her eyes filled with tears. "I'm Sarah," she replied shakily. "I was in the minivan with my kids. They're okay, but I'm just so shaken up. I don't know what to do."

Emma reached out and took Sarah's hand, offering a reassuring squeeze. "You're not alone, Sarah. Let me help you. Can you tell me if there's anything specific you need right now?"

Sarah took a deep breath, trying to steady herself. "I don't know. I'm just scared. My husband is on his way, but I don't have any way to contact him. I don't even know where the kids are."

Emma quickly assessed the situation and decided to take action. "Okay, Sarah, let's get you to a safe place first. I'll make sure you're comfortable and then see if I can find out where your kids are."

Emma helped Sarah to her feet and led her to a nearby area where she could sit down and be away from the immediate chaos. She offered Sarah some water from her own bottle and sat with her, providing a calm and supportive presence.

After a few minutes, Emma approached one of the paramedics and explained Sarah's situation. The paramedic assured her that Sarah's children were being taken care of and that her husband was en route. Emma felt a wave of relief knowing that Sarah's family would soon be reunited.

III. The Unexpected Encounter

WHILE SARAH WAS BEING attended to, Emma decided to stay and help in any way she could. She noticed a small crowd gathering around a young man who was sitting on the grass, his face smeared with blood and his clothes torn. He looked disoriented and in pain, and Emma felt a pang of compassion for him.

She approached the young man, who introduced himself as Tom. "I was driving by and got caught in the wreckage," he said weakly. "I'm not sure what happened, but I feel terrible. I'm not even sure if I have any injuries."

Emma quickly assessed Tom's condition and realized he needed medical attention. She flagged down one of the paramedics and explained Tom's situation. The paramedic agreed to take a look at him and provided some initial treatment.

As Tom was being examined, he looked up at Emma with gratitude. "Thank you for helping me. I don't know what I would have done without you."

Emma smiled warmly. "It's what we're here for. Just hang in there, and everything will be alright."

As the paramedics took Tom away for further evaluation, Emma turned her attention back to Sarah. She remained by her side, offering words of comfort and reassurance. Sarah's husband soon arrived, and the reunion was emotional and heartwarming. Emma felt a sense of fulfillment knowing she had made a difference in someone's life.

IV. A Ripple Effect

AS THE SCENE AT THE accident site began to calm down, Emma decided it was time to head to school. She had spent several hours helping those affected and felt a deep sense of gratitude for the opportunity to serve. The experience had reinforced her belief in the importance of compassion and kindness.

Over the next few days, Emma reflected on the accident and the people she had helped. She learned that Sarah's children had been unharmed, and the family was recovering well. Tom had sustained minor injuries but was expected to make a full recovery. Emma felt a profound sense of relief and happiness knowing that her actions had contributed to their well-being.

Emma's encounter with Sarah and Tom became a topic of discussion in her community. People were inspired by her selflessness and the way she went out of her way to help others. Emma was approached by friends, neighbors, and even strangers who praised her kindness and expressed their admiration.

One evening, as Emma was attending a church service, her pastor, Reverend Mitchell, spoke about the importance of living out one's faith through acts of love and service. Emma listened attentively, feeling a deep connection to the message.

Reverend Mitchell's sermon centered around the parable of the Good Samaritan, emphasizing the importance of showing compassion and kindness to those in need. As he spoke, Emma reflected on her recent experience and how it had been a real-life demonstration of the parable's teachings.

After the service, Reverend Mitchell approached Emma and commended her for her actions. "Emma, I heard about what you did at the accident scene. Your kindness and willingness to help are a true reflection of Christ's love. Thank you for being a living example of what it means to be a Good Samaritan."

Emma was humbled by the praise and felt a renewed sense of purpose. She realized that the act of helping others was not just about the immediate impact but also about inspiring others to follow in her footsteps. Her experience had taught her that even small acts of kindness could have a profound effect on individuals and communities.

V. Continuing the Journey

IN THE WEEKS FOLLOWING the accident, Emma continued to embrace her role as a community member dedicated to helping others. She became involved in various local initiatives aimed at supporting those in need, from organizing charity drives to volunteering at shelters.

Her actions had a ripple effect, inspiring others to become more involved in acts of service and outreach. Emma saw firsthand how one person's kindness could spark a movement of generosity and compassion.

Emma's life was enriched by the connections she made and the difference she was able to create. She found fulfillment in her work and in her commitment to living out her faith through meaningful actions. Her relationship with God grew deeper as she saw the impact of His love in her everyday life.

One evening, as Emma sat quietly in her apartment, she reflected on her journey and the lessons she had learned. She opened her Bible to the Book of James and read a passage that resonated deeply with her:

"Religion that God our Father accepts as pure and faultless is this: to look after orphans and widows in their distress and to keep oneself from being polluted by the world."

Emma felt a sense of peace and contentment, knowing that she had followed her calling and made a positive difference in the world. Her experience had taught her the true meaning of compassion and the power of living out one's faith through acts of kindness.

As she closed her Bible and looked out the window at the twinkling city lights, Emma prayed for continued strength and guidance. She was grateful for the opportunity to serve and to be a vessel of Christ's love. She knew that her journey was ongoing and that there were always more opportunities to show kindness and compassion.

With a heart full of gratitude and a spirit renewed by faith, Emma Thompson continued to walk her path, inspired by the lessons of the Good Samaritan and committed to making a difference in the lives of those she encountered. Her story was a testament to the power of love and the enduring impact of selfless acts of service.

EPILOGUE

The story of Emma Thompson, the modern-day Good Samaritan, became an inspiring example of the impact one person's kindness can have on a community. Her actions were a reminder of the teachings of Christ and the importance of living out one's faith through tangible acts of love and compassion.

Emma's journey was a reflection of the principles found in the parable of the Good Samaritan, illustrating how love and kindness transcend boundaries and bring people together. Her story encouraged others to embrace the spirit of the Samaritan, demonstrating that even in the smallest of acts, the love of Christ can shine brightly and make a lasting difference.

As Emma continued her journey of faith and service, she remained a beacon of hope and inspiration, touching the lives of many and reminding everyone of the profound impact of showing kindness to those in need.

Chapter 15: The Faithful Shepherd

I. A Quiet Beginning

The small town of Willow Creek had always been a place where life moved slowly, with its tightly-knit community living in harmony. Nestled between rolling hills and lush forests, it was a picturesque town that seemed untouched by the chaos of the modern world. At the heart of this tranquil setting stood the Willow Creek Church, a modest yet welcoming building that had been a cornerstone of the community for generations.

Reverend Samuel Bennett, the pastor of Willow Creek Church, had been a part of this community for over a decade. His arrival was serendipitous, as if he had been sent by divine intervention to shepherd the people of Willow Creek. With his kind eyes, gentle demeanor, and unwavering faith, Reverend Bennett quickly endeared himself to the townsfolk. His sermons, rooted in deep spiritual wisdom, offered solace and inspiration to all who listened.

Despite his calm and serene exterior, Reverend Bennett carried a profound sense of responsibility. He viewed his role not merely as a spiritual leader but as a servant to his congregation. He believed that faith should be lived out in practical, meaningful ways, and this belief was the foundation of his ministry.

One crisp autumn morning, as the leaves turned brilliant shades of red and gold, Reverend Bennett prepared for the day's service. He knew that today's sermon was particularly important. It was a special service dedicated to the theme of "Living Faith in Action," a subject close to his heart.

As he entered the church, he was greeted by the familiar faces of his congregation. The pews were filled with families, young and old, all eager to hear his message. The aroma of freshly brewed coffee and the soft murmur of conversation created a warm, inviting atmosphere. Reverend Bennett took a moment to observe the scene, feeling a deep sense of gratitude for the community he served.

II. The Call to Action

THE SERVICE BEGAN WITH the congregation singing hymns of praise, their voices blending together in harmonious worship. Reverend Bennett stood at the pulpit, his heart full of anticipation as he prepared to deliver his sermon. His message was inspired by the parable of the Good Shepherd, a story that illustrated the importance of caring for others with compassion and dedication.

"Today, I want to speak about what it means to be a faithful shepherd," Reverend Bennett began, his voice steady and reassuring. "In John 10:11, Jesus says, 'I am the good shepherd. The good shepherd lays down his life for the sheep.' This passage reminds us of the sacrificial love that we are called to embody in our own lives."

He spoke about the responsibilities of a shepherd, both in biblical times and in the modern world. He emphasized that a shepherd's role was not just about guiding and protecting the flock but also about nurturing and loving them. Reverend Bennett shared stories of people who had made a difference in their communities through acts of kindness, service, and compassion.

"Being a faithful shepherd is not limited to those in religious positions," he continued. "Each one of us has the opportunity to be a shepherd in our own right, to care for those around us, and to live out our faith in tangible ways. Our actions should reflect the love of Christ and the principles of His teachings."

The sermon resonated deeply with the congregation. Many had been touched by Reverend Bennett's message, feeling a renewed sense of purpose and commitment to living out their faith. As the service concluded, Reverend Bennett extended an invitation to anyone who felt called to take practical steps in serving others.

III. A Community Transformed

IN THE WEEKS THAT FOLLOWED, Willow Creek experienced a remarkable transformation. The inspiration from Reverend Bennett's sermon sparked a series of community initiatives and acts of service. The townsfolk began to look beyond their own needs and sought ways to make a positive impact on those around them.

One of the first initiatives was a community food drive organized by the church. Volunteers gathered to collect non-perishable items and distribute them to families in need. The effort was met with overwhelming support from the residents of Willow Creek. People of all ages came together to contribute, and the food drive became a symbol of the town's commitment to living out their faith through action.

Another significant project was the establishment of a local shelter for the homeless. Reverend Bennett, along with a group of dedicated volunteers, worked tirelessly to create a safe haven for individuals and families who had fallen on hard times. The shelter provided not only food and shelter but also counseling and support services to help people get back on their feet.

The church also initiated a mentorship program for at-risk youth, pairing them with positive role models who could offer guidance and encouragement. The program aimed to provide a sense of hope and direction for young people facing challenges and uncertainty.

Reverend Bennett's influence extended beyond the church walls. His commitment to service inspired local businesses and organizations to get involved. Many contributed resources and offered their support to the various community projects. The spirit of generosity and collaboration permeated every corner of Willow Creek.

One evening, as Reverend Bennett walked through the town square, he marveled at the changes that had taken place. The once-quiet streets were now bustling with activity, and the sense of unity and purpose was palpable. He felt a profound sense of fulfillment, knowing that the message of faith and service had taken root in the hearts of his congregation.

IV. Challenges and Triumphs

DESPITE THE OVERWHELMING success of the community initiatives, Reverend Bennett and his congregation faced their share of challenges. Not everyone was immediately receptive to the changes, and there were moments of resistance and skepticism.

Some community members were hesitant to embrace the new programs, questioning their effectiveness and the need for such initiatives. Reverend Bennett addressed these concerns with patience and understanding, emphasizing the importance of faith and perseverance in the face of adversity.

He organized open forums and discussions where people could express their concerns and offer feedback. Through these conversations, Reverend Bennett was able to address misconceptions and build trust within the community. His approach was grounded in empathy and a genuine desire to listen and understand.

One of the most significant challenges came when a severe winter storm hit Willow Creek, causing widespread damage and disruption. Many homes were affected, and the town faced an urgent need for assistance and support.

Reverend Bennett rallied the community, mobilizing volunteers and resources to provide relief to those affected by the storm. The church became a central hub for distributing supplies and offering temporary shelter. The resilience and dedication of the volunteers were a testament to the strength of the community spirit that had been cultivated.

Through these trials, Reverend Bennett's leadership and unwavering commitment continued to inspire those around him. His ability to remain steadfast in the face of adversity demonstrated the true essence of being a faithful shepherd. He encouraged his congregation to lean on their faith and support one another, reinforcing the message of unity and compassion.

V. Legacy of Faith

AS THE YEARS PASSED, the impact of Reverend Bennett's ministry continued to be felt throughout Willow Creek. The community had been transformed by the values of service, kindness, and faith that he had instilled.

The church became a beacon of hope and a center of positive change, reflecting the teachings of Christ in every aspect of its mission.

Reverend Bennett's influence extended beyond the town of Willow Creek. His story was shared with other communities, inspiring individuals and congregations to embrace the principles of faith in action. He was invited to speak at conferences and events, where he shared his experiences and encouraged others to follow in his footsteps.

In his later years, Reverend Bennett reflected on his journey with a deep sense of gratitude. He had seen the fruits of his labor and the transformative power of faith in action. His legacy was not just in the programs and initiatives he had established but in the hearts and lives of the people he had touched.

One spring morning, as he walked through the vibrant, blooming town square, Reverend Bennett felt a profound sense of peace. The community he had served with dedication and love was thriving, and the values he had championed were deeply ingrained in the fabric of Willow Creek.

Reverend Bennett's final sermon before his retirement was a poignant reminder of the journey he had undertaken. He spoke of the importance of continuing to live out one's faith and to be a beacon of light in the world. His words were met with heartfelt applause and expressions of gratitude from the congregation.

As he bid farewell to his beloved community, Reverend Bennett knew that his work was complete. He had fulfilled his calling and had made a lasting impact on the lives of those he had served. His legacy would continue through the actions and deeds of the people of Willow Creek, a testament to the power of faith and the enduring spirit of a faithful shepherd.

EPILOGUE

Reverend Samuel Bennett's story became a symbol of the transformative power of faith and the impact of living out one's beliefs through tangible acts of service. His legacy lived on in the community he had nurtured, inspiring others to embrace the principles of compassion, unity, and dedication.

The town of Willow Creek continued to thrive, guided by the values instilled by Reverend Bennett. The church remained a center of support and outreach, and the community continued to demonstrate the love of Christ through their actions.

Reverend Bennett's life was a testament to the enduring power of faith and the difference one person's unwavering dedication can make. His story served as a reminder that true leadership and service are rooted in love, and that the spirit of a faithful shepherd can inspire others to make a meaningful impact in the world.

As the seasons changed and the years went by, the story of Reverend Samuel Bennett remained a beacon of hope and inspiration. His journey was a testament to the power of faith in action and the enduring legacy of a life lived with purpose and devotion.

Don't miss out!

Visit the website below and you can sign up to receive emails whenever Gregory Allen Parker publishes a new book. There's no charge and no obligation.

https://books2read.com/r/B-A-SLYZB-ITXAE

BOOKS 2 READ

Connecting independent readers to independent writers.

About the Author

Pastor Gregory Allen Parker, a graduate of Trinity Theological Seminary, is a devoted pastor and acclaimed author of Christian fiction. With over two decades of ministry experience, his books explore faith's challenges and triumphs, offering readers inspiring and spiritually rich narratives. Celebrated for his compassionate pastoral care and insightful sermons, Pastor Parker's storytelling reflects his deep understanding of Christian values. When not writing or preaching, he enjoys family time, community volunteering, and the outdoors, continuing to inspire and uplift through his faith and craft.